Blood Garden

By K. A. Alexander

VOICES OF WISDOM, REDEMPTION, AND KINGDOM CREATIVITY

First published by 8 Owls Publishing 2021 in the United States of America for worldwide distribution.

Copyright © 2021 by K. A. Alexander
All rights reserved.

First edition October 2021

K. A. Alexander asserts the moral right to be identified as the author of this work.

It is illegal to copy this book, post it to a website, or distribute it by any other means without permission from 8 Owls Publishing. Small quotes may be used in both written or other media driven platforms if it is noted to have come from this original content using both title and author's name.

Book formatting and book cover by 8 Owls Publishing.

Cover photography credited to LydiaGoolia.
Purchased through iStock by Getty Images #186160316
Original Date: October 8, 2013

ISBN # 978-1-952618-04-8

Acknowledgements

I would like to thank the following:

My Heavenly Father for never leaving or forsaking me, even when I wandered, He never left me alone. 2 Timothy 1:7 saved my life. *I have NOT been given a spirit of fear, but of power, love, and a sound mind.*

My kids, Hollie, Justin, and Rebecca. You kept me centered in a crazy time of our lives. It was during this time when I had the thought," *What would happen if a girl found a hidden door in a library, and decided to find out what was inside?"*

Stacy, Savannah, and Grayson Usher, you were the first to read the adventures in this book. Your encouragement kept me writing this story. Thank you!

Kristene O'Dell, my publisher, for believing that my book needed to come out of me and be in the hands of readers who would benefit from the adventures.

Matthew Manes for helping me see myself in a whole new light. Bright. Like a fireworks display at Disney World on New Year's Eve. It worked.

My many mentors, Kenneth and Gloria Copeland, Creflo Dollar, Terri Savelle Foy, Anthony Robbins, and Jack Canfield, all who taught and propelled me into a Future of Possibilities.

The authors, Frank Peretti and Ted Dekker who helped me realize that I wasn't the only one who saw other beings in this world.

Once again, I want to thank my daughter, Rebecca. You have seen, heard and experienced things children should not have to endure. You pulled me up by the bootstraps, kept me focused on our future, and reminded me that God is in control.

Thank you for helping me vanquish the demons. Huzzah!

This book is dedicated to:

All of you who feel like you don't have a place, a purpose, or a reason for being here.

I'm here to say, "Stop wondering. Or worrying. Or whatever else is keeping you from chasing your destiny. You have a much bigger adventure ahead of you than what you realize.

Grab your weapon. We have dragons to slay."

and

To my dad, Al Alexander, who is already in the Garden.

Table of Contents

Chapter 1: *In the Beginning* — pg. 1

Chapter 2: *The Revelation* — pg. 9

Chapter 3: *Covenant Garden* — pg. 16

Chapter 4: *A History Lesson* — pg. 24

Chapter 5: *First Encounters* — pg. 33

Chapter 6: *New Plans* — pg. 44

Chapter 7: *New Friends* — pg. 52

Chapter 8: *Falling Deeper* — pg. 59

Chapter 9: *Life of the Party* — pg. 68

Chapter 10: *Consequences* — pg. 75

Chapter 11: *Aftermath* — pg. 82

Chapter 12: *Destruction and Salvation* — pg. 90

Chapter 13: *The War for a Single Soul* — pg. 99

Chapter 14: *The Invitation* — pg. 111

Chapter 1

In the Beginning

A pearlescent moon witnessed the scene below. The Commander of the Ranks looked over his troops and surveyed the blood-soaked battlefield. The stench of rotting corpses wafted thick in the air causing a slight upturn at the corner of his scabrous mouth.

He took great pleasure in the filth surrounding this position. The previous battle had been fierce, and his adversaries were beginning to gain ground. He had used every blatant assault maneuver at his disposal and found that his opponents were getting wise to them. So, he decided to deploy the small, sneaky arrows of attack. They seemed to cause the most damage before being discovered and extinguished.

If he had to retake lost ground one inch at a time, so be it. Complete and total devastation was his only objective.

The moonlight glistened like new fallen snow, outlining the still forms of the opposing forces. "Idiots. They cannot stay out of the light. That will be their undoing…" he spat, scratching his scaly flesh.

The razor-sharp blast of a horn rang out over the darkened valley, signaling the beginning of the war. The war for a single soul.

Across the battlefield, a trickle of sweat rolled past Andie's eye. Catching a glint of the milky moonlight, her concentration focused on the open field before them. Being newly promoted in this regiment and knowing what was at stake, she knew she couldn't let her mind wander.

But wander it did. Back to a time when her world was crumbling into a stupid teenage nightmare. Little did she know that all she would learn and experience in this valley would lead her into a war to save so many that had been lost for millennia.

Her thoughts drifted back to that night, the house, and the horrible storm that crashed into her life.

The giant stone house groaned as thunder slammed into it. Bony fingers of lightning raked across the sky. Rain-soaked branches threatened to split from the giant trees, twisting as the wind howled through them. Moonlight cast demonic, shadowy images that prowled around the house.

The gardens were usually quiet havens of peace, but tonight they were flooded by torrents of rain blasting through every rocky pathway. The sudden storm had brought an unexpected chill to the air.

The home was a gift to Katie and her son Jonathan from her Godfather King after her husband's untimely death. King had been a gracious and loving godfather to Katie and Kelly, Andie's aunt, and mother, since their parents' deaths when they were younger.

The grand house was the strangest and most wonderful place Andie had ever seen. She imagined herself a treasure hunter and this house was full of rooms perfect for investigating. Now that she lived with Katie, while her parents settled their divorce, she would be exploring all those rooms.

The home was practically a castle, and she was convinced it was a portal to another world, complete with hidden passageways and secret doors. The dwelling was as ancient as the trees in the garden.

Andie shivered with the howling wind.

She had visited her aunt each summer for years. Katie was exciting and loved going on adventures, but also enjoyed reading in her favorite chair in the incredible library. Katie's only child, Jonathan, was a couple years younger than Andie.

Katie could outwork anyone in her garden and yet she had that 'comfy' type of body, a little soft and squishy. Perfect for hugs and snuggles. Nobody could ever pin her down as a specific type of person. She could be as warm and sweet as a fresh batch of her famous brownies, but then again, she could scare off dangerous strangers with her commanding voice. You didn't mess with Katie.

A grand staircase commanded attention from the center of the majestic house. Gorgeous rugs covered the wide-plank wooden floors. Paintings from the Impressionist masters hung on the vast expanses of walls, along with a few of Katie's own works of art. Furniture from far off and exotic places took up residence in the various rooms, creating an incredibly different ambiance in each space. This was a home that celebrated old-world treasures and new findings equally. Gently, this house drew people into its warm embrace. Anyone who visited here was immediately comfortable and found it difficult to want to leave.

Presently, the house was decorated to the hilt for Christmas. Katie barely waited until the first of November to decorate for the holidays. She pulled out all the decorations and all the stops. Nearly every flat surface was covered with the memories of the past, and a constant introduction of new items yearly. It was a good thing Katie had solar panels installed, because the influx of holiday lights would blow a fuse every time. The place sparkled with wonderment, mystery, and was a sheer delight to the eyes of all who gazed upon the spectacle. Andie and Jonathan loved to stretch out on a great pile of pillows and blankets on the floor in the spacious foyer watching the lights twinkle from every corner of the house while they shared stories.

Everywhere you looked, there were windows. In each window a small candle waited for Christmas. Little windows that were perfect for spying on people coming up the walkway, and large, expansive windows for watching the birds and squirrels playing tag in the garden–all dressed in red and green wreaths and garlands.

In the spring, when the weather was nice, Katie would leave the windows open wide to let the crisp breeze blow through the house. More than once, a sudden rainstorm would catch the drapes fluttering out the openings and soak them completely.

Tonight though, even with the thick, velvet drapes closed over the huge picture windows in the main hall, Andie could tell the storm was growing in intensity. It angrily screamed at the house, causing her to shiver with each explosion of thunder. She could almost imagine the battle cries of a fierce, ongoing war.

There were more doors here than she'd ever seen in any other house. She already knew some of these doors lead to well-appointed bedrooms complete with four poster beds encased by dreamy linens and pillows. Comfy, upholstered chairs sat next to intricately carved wooden tables holding reading lamps and small candy dishes. Other doors led to rooms that were practically empty—maybe a chair and table with a candle in the corner. Everywhere you went, the warm, sweet, cinnamon smell of Christmas greeted you with the promise of a delicious treat waiting in the kitchen.

Andie's favorite room was the magnificent library. The musky scent of aged leather bindings with gold-edged pages and ancient history permeated every inch of the room. Giant bookshelves creaked from the weight of the knowledge held within the pages of the volumes. Strange armor and swords quietly stood guard nearby. Huge leather chairs beckoned to anyone looking for a place to retire.

Framed manuscripts written in an angelic hand hung on the dark wood walls. Trying as hard as she could, Andie could only make out a few words on those pages behind glass. She couldn't pull herself away from them, something there begged to be read. "Someday," she promised herself, "I'll figure it out."

Andie felt a connection to her aunt, and thought it was because of their shared love of reading. However, she never understood her aunt's fascination with weapons. The razor-edged swords were intimidating and had marvelous gemstones embedded in their handles. The shields were emblazoned with a family crest bearing the words: per mare; per terra. The little bit of Latin she had learned helped Andie to decipher those words to mean *of water, of land*.

That accomplishment kept her curiosity piqued enough to keep learning everything she could in this fantastic house, and from this fantastic person. Andie wanted to learn everything about anything, mainly because it distracted her from the misery of her own world. More than anything else, she wondered about a massive wooden door that seemed out of place in this spacious library. It stood there, a quiet sentinel, keeping a secret unto itself.

The storm continued its assault outside their safe haven while two sets of soulless eyes watched silently from the darkness.

Thankfully, the books provided a much-needed escape and Andie enjoyed them in her favorite chair, getting lost in their worlds. These were worlds where she could be the hero of a treacherous quest; or maybe a genius detective discovering the hidden clue; or simply learn a few lost details in history. In her "real" world, Andie felt left out and unwanted.

She wasn't a 'stand out' type of person and wasn't likely to be voted for the student council or prom queen. Andie was pretty, in a quiet, reserved way. The long brown hair that matched her eyes was eclipsed by her shy smile. Her one claim to fame was her unerring ability to perfectly apply her winged eyeliner. No matter what else she struggled with, she could always depend on her silly eyeliner to make her feel like she did something right.

Another bolt of lightning exploded in the sky, triggering the thunder crashing into the walls of her fortress. "Seriously, I swear I can hear all hell breaking loose out there…" whispering to nobody in particular.

The two sets of eyes looked at each other, nodding in agreement. It was indeed breaking loose.

She was trying to ignore the screeching winds outside the windows, and while shuffling through the books on the shelves looking for yet another adventure, an envelope fell to the floor. Picking it up, Andie noticed it felt wonderfully weighty, possibly from an elegant, vintage personal stationery. She turned it over and read the name written across the front, catching her breath…

"To my dearest Andie"

A warm rush of anticipation raced through her body. The rest of the room faded away as she fumbled for a chair. Even the raging storm outside seemed to subside. Trembling, she gently opened the envelope and pulled out the most beautiful handwritten letter she had ever seen, and yet, somehow the writing seemed familiar to her. The words both thrilled and amazed her. The person who wrote the letter spoke to her every thought and fear. When Andie read the letter, the words jumped off the paper and into her heart. A portion of that letter follows:

*"My beloved, I have been calling to you
and now it is time for you to learn
of the things I have waited years to tell you.*

*I knew you had to reach a point in your life
where I had your full attention,
and recent events have caused you to lose faith
in the world around you.*

*You are called to be a woman of strength,
courage, and honor.*

*Now, Andie, you will begin your journey
into a world where you are one of my warriors."*

It was signed, *"Your Faithful, Loving
Godfather King"*

Slowly, Andie laid the letter in her lap. Her heart was racing, her thoughts were scattered, but one thing was clear, she had to find Katie. Maybe she could explain this letter. First, she had to make her legs carry her out of the room.

-... .-.. --- --- -..

The elder spoke to the younger, "You know your mission."

"Yes.' replied the subordinate, "This one MUST NOT be allowed to take her place."

"You also know the penalty for failure."

The younger gulped, "Yes, my prince."

Chapter 2

The Revelation

Katie!
The word was barely out of Andie's mouth when she turned the corner to the kitchen and plowed into her aunt. Catching her breath, she asked, "Do you know anything about this?"

Katie read the letter, then smiled as she handed it back and said, "Honey, I think we need to have a little talk."

"*I haaate when people say that…* " Andie thought, rolling her eyes, but she HAD to know what this meant. She went to the kitchen table, pulled out a chair and plopped down.

Katie poured a glass of milk to go with the warm, gooey brownies. The storm was still raging outside, and it seemed to direct its fury at the house. Andie was convinced the torrential storm would tear the house apart. She couldn't remember a storm this bad in all the years she came to visit.

Tonight, was different. There was electricity in the air around them, the kind that causes the hair on your arms to stand up. It was clear that even as the storm clawed at the house, the house would withstand the attack. Andie was still convinced there was a war going on outside.

"Ok, now, let me tell you a few things about our Godfather King." Katie started as she sat across the table. Her words were soothing but had an edge. She knew a fierce secret that wasn't going to be easy to explain. "We have a family ancestry that goes back thousands of years, and not all of it is pretty," she continued. "I've known for years you would come to a place in time where you would learn this, and I'm honored to be the one to help you."

The wind screamed at the windows causing the shutters to beat against the casings.

Katie looked deep into Andie's eyes and saw that the time was right to reveal the truth to her niece. "Honey, we are a family of warriors in a world of unseen creatures, some are pure and strong and fight with us against our enemy–an enemy who is vicious and hellbent on our destruction." She smoothed out a wrinkle on the tablecloth.

A flash of lightning threatened to cut out the power causing the lights to flicker. She let the words sink in for a moment. Andie didn't even blink. Never broke eye contact with her aunt. "*That's about right...*" Katie mused, "Andie, are you ok?"

Andie set the brownie down onto the plate, wiped the crumbs from her fingers and nodded her head a little, answering, "Uh huh, I thought I heard you say that we are a family of warriors. Do you mean like knights in shining armor, or more like ninja warriors, *ha-ha*...?" It wasn't a natural laugh; it was kind of forced. Unsure of her aunt's meaning, Andie looked to see if she was laughing as well.

Katie wasn't smiling. Andie's smile quickly melted.

"You're serious, aren't you?" Andie asked, narrowing her gaze.

"Our family, under the guidance of Godfather King, has been fighting a battle in an unseen world for centuries. I think you are aware, in some confusing way, that there is something more to your life than just going to school, dealing with your parents, and doing chores." Katie tried to be gentle, but there are some instances that are simply difficult to explain.

Andie laid her head down on her crossed arms, and desperately sought for a handle in her mind to regain her balance. The events of the past few months had been weighing heavy on her heart.

Andie thought back to the beginning of the latest trauma. She had no idea her smile was what attracted Brian. It took him several days to finally talk to her, and several weeks to ask her out. They only dated for a short time, just hanging out at the library, or the park. But having someone to talk to had been a dream come true. One of the most devastating things Andie ever experienced was learning of the car wreck that claimed his young life. After that, she clung to her friend Carla, for dear life.

Carla was the best friend a girl could hope to have in her life. Being the oldest sibling wasn't always easy, but having a best friend like Carla, made life a little better. Andie and Carla found each other at the beginning of middle school and no force on earth could separate them. That is, until their junior year of high school when Carla's dad relocated to a job halfway across the state. They made plans to spend school breaks with each other, but with Andie's parents divorcing, Carla hadn't been allowed to visit until things were settled. So now, Andie felt very much alone without either of her friends close by to share her secrets and heartaches. Ugh. She hated that feeling.

"Dear God, what else could possibly happen..." She cried to herself on many sleepless nights. Truthfully, she didn't really

want to know what else could go wrong. All this torment had to end soon, or she wouldn't be able to handle life anymore.

"Andie, this is a safe place for you to tell me your fears and your dreams." Katie was hoping she would get a response from Andie soon. She knew about the misfortunes that had affected her niece. "*Please, help me not scare her off.*" Katie whispered as Andie looked across the table.

"Let me see if I've got this straight," moving the plate of brownies away from her. "After everything that has happened in the past year, you want me to believe that we are some kind of "*warriors*", (her fingers making air quotes), and we fight against ghostly creatures?" Andie asked, sarcasm dripping from every word.

"Yes," Katie was resolute.

"AUGH! You're crazy..." Andie barked, smacking her hand on the table.

"*Good. She doesn't believe it.*" *A sly smile crawled across the face with the soulless eyes.*

Katie just smiled, settled into her chair, and said, "No, I'm not crazy, and yes, we are warriors, along with a few other things that you will learn about later."

Andie squinted at her aunt, halfway expecting the theme music from 'The Twilight Zone' to be playing. It wasn't. Katie had a solid look of resolve on her face. Andie had never seen her aunt appear this serious before now.

"So, what am I supposed to do, 'go on a quest' or something?" Andie offered. After no response from Katie, she continued, "Seriously!?"

Still no response from Katie.

"I don't have a choice, do I?" Andie demanded.

"Of course, you have a choice, but you have to understand that the only way you will ever settle the storm in your heart is to take this information and follow through with it," Katie replied. "Do you remember when you asked me about that door in the library? Well, now is the time for you to make the decision to find out what's there or live with this heartache and pain for the rest of your life. *That* is your choice."

Katie hadn't answered any questions about the door, and the feeling that crept into Andie's heart when she went near the door was both exciting and frightening at the same time. She wanted to explore, but then again, maybe not...

"Now that you live here with me, you are free to go into any room, look through anything you want or need. I know you will find the nerve to go through the door that you've spent so many hours thinking about, and in there, you will find your answers. Trust me when I tell you that you can talk to me about ANYTHING, no matter how strange or silly it may seem to you." Katie spoke in a tone that was gentle yet firm.

"OK, thanks..." was all Andie could muster in a numb response.

Katie left Andie alone to think about all this for a while as she started supper. Andie distractedly went through the motions of setting the table. Katie shared a smile with Jonathan as they watched Andie eating, lost in thought.

After saying "good night" to Katie and Jonathan, Andie sat in her chair in the library in her night clothes and house shoes, staring at the door. The chill was still thick in the air from the storm raging outside.

"Do not fail. I don't have to remind you of the eternal torment you will endure, do I?"

"No, my prince. I remember."

-... .-.. --- --- -..

The library was dimly lit from the slowly dying fireplace as Andie made her way to the door in the far corner. "Good grief, you're being stupid," Andie said out loud at her reluctance to open the door. "You know you *want* to; you *need* to, you *have to see* what Katie was talking about. After all, it's just a door, right? What could possibly happen?" Famous last words.

Right on cue, lightning flashed casting eerie shadows around the room and thunder rumbled through the house rattling light fixtures and pictures on the walls. "You're NOT helping!" she yelled to the storm and reached for the brass doorknob. It was cool to her touch.

Obeying the command from her fingers, the knob silently turned and opened the door. A long, narrow hallway stretched into the abyss. A warmth flushed through her as she stepped over the threshold. When her eyes adjusted to the darkness from the door closing behind her, she could see the outline of another door at the far end. The hallway smelled damp, kind of mildewy, and she didn't dare touch the walls. She didn't realize it right away, but the roar of the storm outside subsided. ~Slightly~

She fussed at herself for not bringing a flashlight, and more than once, she stumbled on a rug on the floor. At least, she hoped it was a rug, she didn't dare take her eyes off the hairline of light stretching around the far door. Andie had never been a big fan of the dark, and right now wasn't the time to get distracted. The darkness was thick as mud.

Horrible thoughts teased her brain. "*What if you get lost in here? Maybe the reason you were told to come in here was to 'get lost' for good. You don't need to go any farther. Nobody will be able to find you. You're not even sure they will come looking for you... Maybe you should go catch up on your television show, the finale is next week...*"

She started to tremble from the torturous thoughts racing in her head. "*Give up and go back, you don't really need to go any farther, turn back.... You're not ready for what happens next. You should wait until you're older, thinner, prettier, smarter.* **GET OUT OF HERE***!*"

She felt those last words, and began to wonder if she should turn back, climb in bed, and watch television. "*Go back, you don't belong here."*

"Dear God, does this torment ever end?" Andie whispered as she stumbled through the darkened hallway. As the words left her lips, there was the sound of a wind rushing around her, the air smelled sweeter and felt warmer as Andie began to see the door ahead more clearly. Holding her breath, she reached for the crystal doorknob.

It was warm to her fingers. She turned the handle and pushed gently. A glimmer of light shone upon a gold name plate on the door inscribed with the words, 'Covenant Garden.' She smiled, pushed a little more, and squinted her eyes in anticipation of what she would find inside.

The storm outside went silent.

Chapter 3

Covenant Garden

Blinking through squinted eyes, she stepped through the door into golden sunlight bathing an emerald-green valley in a gentle warmth. Andie turned to look at the door, standing by itself on top of a hill, massively damaged and bearing scars from a prolonged battle at its threshold. It reminded her of how the house resisted the furious storm.

Andie turned to face the sunlight, she closed her eyes and slowly tilted her head back. Letting the warmth wash over her, she felt a lifetime of fear, rejection and hurt melt off like wax exposed to heat. Andie was surprised how peaceful she felt. She let her shoulders relax as she deeply breathed in the fragrant air. A cool breeze wafted across her face, teasing her hair.

Her thoughts returned to the letter in the library and wondered if this was the journey that was mentioned. A calm voice in her heart assured her she was right, and she would never be lost again. This was the place she had been searching for all her life.

"So, Katie knew about this and that's why she said that I needed to find out for myself what was on the other side." Then the thought

struck her, Katie had been here and knew how wonderful it felt to be this peaceful.

After a few moments of reflection, Andie slowly opened her eyes. The best way she could describe what she saw was...

The soft blue sky, dotted with fluffy, delicate clouds paled in comparison to the sapphire depths of the stream. The water rushed past tender green grass bending in the caress of the fragrant breeze. Everything, so full of life, pulsed with color in this expansive garden valley.

Her senses were quickly becoming overwhelmed. She looked around for the source of the music floating through the air. Andie could only guess the entire place was alive with this glorious song that filled her ears and flooded her heart.

The wind gently teased her hair, and she closed her eyes in sweet surrender. She raised her arms out to embrace the warmth of the sunlight, and for the first time in her life, Andie felt truly alive.

"I've waited so long for you," a gentle voice interrupted her reverie.

She jumped and screamed, swinging out her arm in defense at the unknown source of the voice. She had been so lost in the wonderment of the sheer beauty of this place, just hearing another person speak scared her senseless. Quickly, she turned around to face the most extraordinary person she had ever seen. Andie's heart pounded so hard; she was positive he heard it. He smiled as he apologized for startling her, walked over, and placing his hands on her shoulders he tenderly kissed her on the forehead. Andie was dumbstruck with awe.

His laugh sparkled, reminding her of a delicate wind chime but at the same time, she heard a strength and authority deep inside. His short black hair was sprinkled with gray throughout, and his face, tanned with experience, had a youthfulness about it. His smiling eyes reflected the sky, the earth, and the depth of untold joy. Even though his hands were gentle, they held a hidden strength. She knew he could catch her if her legs gave way.

He was dressed simply in a tunic and pants with slip-on shoes. His gentle demeanor caused Andie to relax, and she realized this had to be the person who wrote the letter– Godfather King. There was no other explanation.

Through the amazement of all the things surrounding her, Andie began to have a new respect for Katie. There were still plenty of things that she didn't know about her favorite aunt.

"I will never get tired of seeing that expression. One of surprise mixed with shock. It's always the first look people have on their face as they meet me here in Covenant," he explained, extending his hand. A brilliantly colored butterfly had flitted around their heads before landing on the back of his open hand. Andie marveled as she realized the colored wings not only shimmered in the glorious sunlight but sparkled like cut jewels.

In that slow-motion daze you feel during periods of intense stress or elation, Andie was positive she heard the rush of the wind as the butterfly took flight. She noticed Godfather King was watching her as she turned to watch it fly away.

He reassured her, "Right now you feel like you're in shock, but as you learn more about this place, this will become normal for you."

"The wind you hear is actually the Life Source of this place, without it, all would cease to exist." He waved his arm in a sweeping motion as he continued, "It is the reason you came through the door and the reason you feel at peace now. It has been pulling at you for some time, trying to get your attention in your 'real world.' This is a place of safety and peace where my warriors and soldiers come together."

She really did feel peaceful. All the pain from before had drained from her heart and mind. As she breathed a sigh of relief, she noticed the thousands of soldiers surrounding them. Peaceful and serene, yet completely ready for battle, these fighters were as timeless as their King.

This King—the butterfly befriending person in front of her was watching her again. He smiled as he spoke, "You will find many wonderful things here, but you have also come here to prepare for battle."

Andie's mind went blank. *"Wait. What?"*

"You are so much stronger than you realize. If you will keep your focus on me and what I teach you, you will be able to accomplish more than you ever thought possible." Andie could feel his words as well as hear them. She knew he was telling her the truth. He continued, "These are my soldiers and have special tasks assigned to them. You will learn to fight along with them, but because I have called you, you will become a great leader in this army."

"Even though you will fight an enemy that is older than time itself and has prevailed on this planet for thousands of years, you already have the Victory. You will need to remind him of that fact constantly. He will not rest or refrain from causing you heartache and pain. His only desire is to deceive or destroy everyone he can find. He is full of lies and will incessantly try to fill your heart and mind with his filth. If you speak and act like me, he will see me. If you don't, then he will see you and retaliate against you even harder than before," Godfather King stated, letting his words settle in her racing mind.

"He loathes you with a venomous hatred unlike anything you have ever imagined. Long before you were aware of it, he was eating away at your heart, trying to cause you to lose hope and fall into despair." Andie began to realize he was referring to several times in her life that she truly felt like she wanted to die. Images of her friends and her family returned along with the familiar pain. Her heart began to hurt again.

"Andie, you've had a powerful warrior fighting for your safety and protection." He smiled when he saw the look of recognition come over her face.

"Yes, Katie is one of the strongest warriors in this army. The enemy didn't stand a chance against her. She knows exactly who she is and what she can do in my authority. The enemy has suffered greatly because she is relentless. I find great joy in watching her and listening to her wage war on the filth he expels toward you." He went on to say, "and that is the same power and authority you now possess. I look forward to watching both of you."

All that Andie could do was stare, then slowly blink and stare again. "*Wow, this is going to take some time to figure out...*" she thought to herself, breaking her stare, and shaking her head.

"Don't worry, understanding will come. I am so happy that you're here and we can spend time together now," Godfather King said happily.

Confusion spread across Andie's face.

"Oh yes, I can hear your thoughts," King said, smiling at this revelation.

"*Oh great,*" she thought, rolling her eyes.

The King laughed and took her hand. "Come, I want to show you something," he said, pulling her close to his side.

The sound of the wind increased, the surroundings blurred and before she could blink, they were standing on a windy mountaintop. "Look as far as your eyes will let you," King whispered, still holding her near. The view was breathtaking, unlike anything Andie had ever seen. The colors were so much brighter here, and she could see details of distant, delicate flowers. She was certain the grass would feel like silk if she could just slip her shoes off.

"*I can see for miles...*" she thought.

"What may seem like miles to you is merely an arm's reach for me," he revealed, smiling at her amazement.

"Come again..." and they were off once more. This time they stood on a powdery soft beach, waves lapping before their feet.

"How deep do you think it is?" he asked. After the last trip, she knew she couldn't dare guess. "This is but a teardrop in comparison to how deep my love is for my beloved ones." Soaring gulls called out overhead. Turquoise colored waves crashing against the nearby boulders sent sparkling sprays of foam high in the air. He winked at her and with a smile he hinted, "One more time..."

The movement was astronomical.

Yes, that's how she would describe it. How else do you explain floating weightlessly in the pitch-black nothingness of space?

The King smiled as he declared, "It's not a '*nothingness*' as you discern it. It's full of life and breath, look again." This time he waved his hand in front of her as if to hold back an invisible veil. She gasped as her eyes saw things that you can only conjure in your dreams of the empyreal universe. Stars, planets, moons, galaxies, winged creatures—limitless sight was granted to her for a moment. Andie squeezed him as she tried to soak up the unbelievable beauty of the celestial scene.

"Don't be afraid, Andie, I am always with you, closer than your heartbeat." With this statement, he held her tighter, and in a blink, they were once again in the place they started.

"What.Was.THAT!?" she squeaked, still shaking, still clinging on for dear life.

King smiled and replied, "I simply wanted to show you some of the things I've created for you. From the smallest dewdrop to the farthest reaches of the universe," he paused and smiled, "and much more than I can show you right now. All of this was designed and created simply for you to enjoy with me."

"*But HOW in the world...?*" the thoughts scrambled through her brain.

"My words have the ability to bring about Life. You will have the opportunity to put that into action soon."

"*Ha, yeah right.*" she thought to herself, forgetting that he could hear her thoughts.

"Andie, you have to understand that the words you speak have the same power I used to create all this, and so much more," then King urgently stated as he faced her, "If you don't completely and totally put your trust in me, then you cannot be as effective in your mission as you truly need to be. And you run the risk of being destroyed by the enemy."

"Nothing is impossible for me, and the same is true for you. I can stop the earth's orbit around the sun. I can cause the rain to fall unhindered for weeks on end. I have created and named each of those glorious stars that shine continually for you, even when you don't see them."

"I have set laws into motion in this universe, and I follow them as I expect all others to follow them, but I am not bound by them. Gravity, day and night, seed time and harvest will continue all the days of this earth. I am able to move through time and space because I created them.

There are stones of creation that you will acquire in your journey. These stones will become medals of Honor and Valor for which you will be recognized as a Warrior Leader. The first was given when you came through the door," King explained, "the Emerald is for long life. Your heart will never die now that you've come back to me. The Diamond is for clarity and strength, which you demonstrated in the recent events involving your family and friends. So, now you have the stones that represent Eternal Life and Strength."

Andie wasn't exactly sure what to think about all this new information, and when King saw her confusion, he said, "When you return home, you will see what I'm talking about, Andie."

Her heart raced when he spoke her name. She felt cherished as she heard her name through his voice. A gentle, yet overwhelming feeling of peace filled her from head to toe. He was beginning to win her heart.

Then his face turned serious, he placed his hands on both her shoulders as he leaned closer to her, and said, "We have to hurry Andie, the gates will be closing soon and there are so many people left to reach."

"*What is he talking about, and WHY does he need me to help him?*" It shouldn't have surprised her when he answered, but it did.

Chapter 4

A History Lesson

My loved ones were exiled from my kingdom several millennia ago because they chose to believe the devastating, ruinous lies of a traitor. He promised them everything they could ever want if they listened to him. A kingdom-splitting deception took place because the enemy wanted to tear my heart open and destroy the ones I love. Only those who have come back to me can reach the ones who are lost.

"How did this happen?" Andie asked.

A look of deep sorrow filled his face as his shoulders sagged. A cool breeze engulfed them, and Andie began to regret asking the question.

Breathing in slowly and squaring his shoulders, King responded, "Long ago, one of my most trusted officers decided he wanted more. Everything he ever needed was supplied at his request. But because of his station in the kingdom, greed grew in his heart, and he began to think that he should be on the throne. I couldn't allow this to happen. There was more at stake than just the throne. My family and friends were at risk of being annihilated."

"Immediately, I had the usurper and his followers permanently banished from my realm. Nearly a third of my own army had pledged their allegiance and vowed to fight alongside him. I couldn't allow division to enter my kingdom." Soldiers standing nearby nodded in agreement.

"As a result," King continued, "the traitor fabricated lies, causing doubt among the dearest people in my kingdom, my family. They were tricked into leaving the safety of my care and protection. You can't imagine how devastating it was to me. It took many years for a plan to be put into effect to redeem those who left and to bring them home again. By the time the plan could be put into action, the descendants of the early defectors had grown to an innumerable population."

"Thousands upon thousands have returned home, but there are many still in danger. I want every one of them to be given the choice to return to me. I will receive them with open arms. Their other choice is to continue listening to the lies and forever be exiled from my kingdom." He confessed, "I will give them everything they need if they will simply return to me. It is my deepest desire that all return." Andie could feel his genuine concern for all those who were lost, and it pulled on her heart. A tall, dark-skinned soldier put his hand over his heart and lowered his head.

"A plan came together. It was my choice, and it was excruciating, but it was the only way to resolve the situation. I gave up my life as an offering to the enemy. I willingly allowed the enemy to do to me all that was in store for the ones he deceived, even unto death. The enemy celebrated his victory, thinking I had been defeated, but he didn't understand the power of sacrifice. When an innocent person forfeits his life for another, powerful forces are released. It was all planned from the beginning, he had to believe he won. He was so blinded by his rage and apparent victory to think it through."

"Even though I told them beforehand what had to happen, my friends were tormented. Imagine their shock and surprise when I walked back into the room and declared a way had been made for the return of the lost, and the total defeat of the enemy had been secured." King smiled at the memory and continued, "The lost ones would have to be found and told of the reprieve. The only condition was the people would have to make the decision to return or be lost forever. Nothing could be forced on them, they had to *want* to come home." This statement caused a stir among the troops.

Andie felt as though her heart would crumble, wondering, *"How could anyone NOT come to someone who loves them so much that he willingly let his enemy torture and execute him?"* She couldn't keep her eyes off him. There were no outward signs of trauma, but she could hear the pain in his voice. There was a calmness in the breeze, caressing her hair, causing her to relax.

King went on to say, "The enemy still tries to poison their minds by reminding them they left once, and now they don't deserve to return. He will fight until the last moment to keep them from returning to me. It is your mission to fight for the safety of those who haven't returned; and to support those who have returned and are now under attack."

"Words are weapons, and that is how the enemy tricked my loved ones—with his deceitful words," explained King. "Have you noticed how your heart soars when someone says something uplifting, or how painful it is when someone says something hurtful? They do not realize the power in their words, and they don't use them wisely. When the correct words are used in wisdom and authority, you can defeat the enemy, and you can cause miraculous events to come to pass."

"However, if you aren't diligent in guarding your words, they can be used to bring forth a negative effect as well," he cautioned Andie. "These soldiers respond to commands given in my authority, but they can't or won't respond to words spoken in fear or anger. Those are the words the enemy uses to his advantage. Keep watch over your heart to make sure what you say and do isn't done out of spite or malice."

"You have already seen some of these soldiers in your world. You didn't know them, but they knew you; and fulfilled their commission of protecting and guiding you. After you learn more of your place here, you will begin to see more of them in your world. As well as the agents of the enemy. Yes, they fight against you there, too," King informed her. "The storm that raged war at Katie's house is just one example of his work. It was an effort to scare you—to prevent you from coming here. I knew you were braver and stronger than anything he would throw at you."

Memories came rushing back to Andie. Thoughts of someone always interrupting her and 'just wanting to sit and talk' or 'needing directions.' But she couldn't put a face on any of them now. *"Could they have been...?"* she wondered. Piercing green eyes from the nearest soldier penetrated her thoughts, and he seemed strangely familiar. He smiled at her.

"Yes, they were sent to protect you, and did what they could to redirect your thoughts," King answered her thoughts aloud.

"I wish I had been more aware of what was going on," Andie replied wistfully.

"Well, now you are aware, and you are responsible for what you know," he reminded her. "Great consideration should be used when speaking in my authority. Your words must line up with mine. Only then will you have complete dominion over the enemy."

"You will be learning more every hour, every day; and as your knowledge increases, you will see your reinforcements, as well as the enemy, in the 'real world'." A blond, youthful looking soldier nodded when Andie looked at him.

King warned her, "You must never let your guard down. The enemy knows the threat that you present to him, and he will do anything and everything possible to distract or stop you." King paused, "He will try to kill you."

Soldiers surrounding them stood motionless, resolute in their stance.

"I have given you the ability to speak with my authority, but you have to trust in me for this to do you any good. You have been given the Grace to act and speak like me. That is the difference between you and the ones we need to find." King looked deep into her eyes.

"Okay..." was all Andie could manage to say, feeling anxious and overwhelmed.

"Don't worry, you'll be fine. In the middle of the battle, Wisdom will come, Peace will find you, and Victory will be in your hand. There are several challenges that you will have to face to become the warrior for which you are destined.

"Remember in whose Authority you operate, and remember, you'll never be alone, Andie. I am always nearby. You can cause things to happen that you haven't even thought of yet." King spoke softly, but she could feel the depth of his words penetrating her heart and mind.

A little spark of curiosity flickered in her heart, causing her to wonder just what he meant, but this entire event had taken its toll on her. She was exhausted and wasn't sure she could remember everything she'd been taught.

Godfather King sensed her fatigue and reassured her that it would all still be fresh to her when she needed to call on it. He held her close again and gently told her goodnight. Once again, the gentle breeze caressed her face.

The most peaceful sleep engulfed her. She sighed in relief and surrendered to the slumber creeping into her body. A small part of her brain registered the coolness of the air and the sheets as she snuggled in her bed. She'd worry about how she got home tomorrow.

Andie couldn't remember ever sleeping as well as she did that night. At first, what seemed like a strange, anxiety induced dream came back to her. She roused herself convinced that it really did happen. How else could she have seen some of those marvelous sights, heard the melodious voice of her Godfather King and felt a tremendous weight lift from her heart if it had been only a dream? She couldn't help but smile while she got dressed, thinking, "*Katie is going to freak out when I tell her what I saw!*"

Katie and Jonathan had fixed breakfast when Andie came bounding down the staircase. Smiling to each other, they were thrilled that Andie finally went through the door.

Katie only smiled and nodded as Andie's words spilled forth in a gush of energy. Andie stopped babbling and looked at her aunt. "You knew what was going to happen, didn't you?" she questioned.

"Of course!" was the reply, "But would you have believed me if I tried to tell you all that without you seeing it first?"

"No, I probably would have looked up the phone number for a hospital," Andie teased.

"So, you agree this 'crazy' lady has plenty of things to teach you?" Katie asked.

"I'm sorry for calling you crazy. I couldn't think of any other explanation for what you were telling me. Now I know better." Andie apologized, hugged Katie, and sat down to eat.

For the first time in years, Andie felt like she could take anything the world could dish out. A thought popped into her head, "What can you tell me about the sacrifice?" The hair on her arms stood out and she saw Katie's smile disappear. Jonathan stopped eating. Even the house seemed morose. "*Hmm, THAT struck a nerve...*" she thought, furrowing her brow.

Without speaking, Katie led Andie to the library. Once there, Katie showed her a new sword that she realized had not previously been showcased. It had a gorgeous diamond and an emerald embedded in the handle. Katie smiled as she walked over to the wall where the beautiful handwritten letters were hanging. Jonathan helped her gently lift one of the massive, wooden frames off the wall and carried it to a table in the corner while Andie quickly cleared it off.

Standing there quietly, Andie began to realize that she could now read the exquisite script lettering. After a few moments of reading, she began to cry. Katie held her close and told her that it was the worst thing she had ever read in her life, too. Like a treasure hidden in plain sight, this letter chronicling the King's pain and suffering was heart wrenching. Somehow her whole body felt the sadness. Jonathan wrapped his arms around them both.

Now, she was glad for not being able to read this before she met Godfather King. She felt a deepening respect and loyalty to him. As she read, her heart became more resolved to do anything he asked of her.

Andie wasn't sure how to deal with the feelings of sadness and pain that now clouded her thoughts. The recounting of the torture, beatings, and eventual death of this person she had recently met and come to trust, haunted her everywhere she went during the day.

As days passed, Andie became more determined to do whatever she could to be sure all the pain and suffering wouldn't be in vain. The more she thought about helping King, the more she realized she wanted to know more about him personally. "*What kind of person, even a king, would go through such horrible events to make a way for people who had rejected him in order to return home?*" That was the biggest question she had to have answered. With that thought in mind, she determined she would ask him.

Andie spent an afternoon looking through the expansive selection of books dedicated to swordplay and hand to hand combat. More than once, she giggled to herself realizing her choice of reading was vastly different than just a few days ago.

Andie spent many days in Covenant Garden with King, soaking up anything and everything he said. He told her stories of his eternal realm and some from her past. She was amazed at how whenever she thought she was near the end of her rope with her family, friends, and school, he had been there, watching, speaking to her heart, encouraging her to not give up.

At times, she felt like a silly little girl, with messy hair, her bare feet and legs covered in mud, her face covered in smiles. She felt more alive every second she spent with King. Other times, she truly did feel like she was becoming a soldier, strong and sure of herself.

Her affection for him grew with each passing lesson. She saw him as a kind Godfather but at the same time, she felt a reverence for him as one does for a person of experience and intelligence. She began to refer to him as King and was slightly surprised when nobody reacted any differently. Never had she known someone as gentle and caring, and yet so resolute in his authority. She was treated as one the group when she trained with the soldiers. They were always ready to show her how to improve something she questioned.

She grew in her ability to fight with her sword, sometimes training with Jonathan, sometimes with King, and random spars with a passing soldier kept her on her toes. Her confidence grew and the doubts that haunted her mind shriveled with each passing day. She began to crave and seek out time to spend in the garden with her King. This felt like home.

Chapter 5

First Encounters

A little past midnight, Andie sat straight up in bed breathing hard, as an unholy sound screeched through her dreams causing adrenaline to pound in her veins. "WHAT was THAT!?" she whispered in the darkness. Inexplicably, she felt an overwhelming urge to rush back to the garden and find out what was going on. Still in her pajamas, she took off running for the door.

Katie whispered a prayer as she turned off the lights. She had heard Andie cry out in her sleep, and she hoped that Andie could handle what she was about to encounter.

Although she had never felt it before, Andie had a strange desire to hit something, and hit it HARD! She slowed her pace as she neared the door, unsure of what she would find on the other side. Once again, the doorknob obeyed her touch and opened to the darkened hallway. A rush of adrenaline had flushed her cheeks, warmth spreading down her throat. Andie noticed the light from the far door at the other end of the hall wasn't as bright as she remembered from her first visit. Fighting the choking feeling rising in her throat, she cautiously opened the door and stepped into Covenant.

The sky was dark with thick clouds rolling in waves. Fear gripped her and she was shaking. Andie had never seen anything like this and wasn't sure what she should do when, yet another scream pierced the darkness.

Her eyes spied a wretched fiend racing towards her cousin, Jonathan, standing several yards away from her. The beast grabbed the boy around the waist, flung him over its shoulder and ran at an unbelievable speed. The boy screamed as he looked back at Andie. A shriek of disbelief escaped her throat, and she took up pursuit. As she ran, she noticed there was a sword in her hand. She gripped it tightly, assured that she was comfortable enough to use it.

The beast towered near nine feet tall and was built like a grotesque version of a horror movie monster with many different body parts pieced together. It was covered in a mangy, greasy, fur-like hide, and stank like the worst skunk roadkill she could possibly imagine.

She was sick to her stomach thinking about how close the boy was to the head of the monster. It could have bitten him in half. The demon's huge talon-like claws dug up the earth as it ran unfathomably fast.

"What in the world is THAT?!" she would have screamed if she had the breath left to say anything. Andie had no intention of letting this filthy monster get away with the boy. She would destroy the beast to get Jonathan back. Her heart ached for her cousin.

As Andie chased after them, her legs began to hurt, her lungs were burning from the exertion, and she could feel her pulse pounding in her ears. She would die before she gave up. She was close enough to see the boy's eyes and wished desperately that she could rescue him.

Like a bolt from the blue, a thought struck her, *"Use your weapon…"*

"DROP HIM!" she demanded. Andie was almost surprised to see that the beast stopped while tightening its enormous fist around the boy. As it turned around and faced Andie, a cruel sneer stretched across its foul, foaming mouth exposing yellowed fangs, then it bellowed with an unholy roar as it forcefully drove a jagged weapon into the boy's chest.

Andie slid to a stop; horror frozen on her face. The boy went pale and crumpled to the ground. The beast raised the stained blade over his head fully intending to plunge it into the boy again. It let out a blood curdling howl that sent shivers down Andie's spine, their eyes met, and she saw the beast was filled with evil, spewing hatred.

"NO! LEAVE HIM ALONE!" Andie screamed and started running for the boy. The beast turned and ran into the darkness. She could still hear it's vicious screeching as it disappeared.

The stench lingered and forcefully gagged her. Andie fell to her knees next to Jonathan. She could tell he was bleeding profusely from the hole in his chest and had only moments to live. As Andie started to panic, the wind swirled around the two of them causing her to focus and relax. Firmly gripping the boy with her arm, she laid the hilt of her sword in her hand on his chest and spoke barely louder than a whisper, saying, "Bleeding, you will stop, and wound, you will close NOW by the authority of the King..."

Gently rocking and crying, Andie held him in her lap, wishing there was more she could do for him. The breeze swirled around them again, bringing a freshness to the air.

The boy stirred. He inhaled deeply, causing Andie to jump. He slid his hand over his chest, to the place where the bleeding had been the worst. His fingers feeling the bloody stickiness that soaked his shirt. She couldn't help staring in wide-eyed wonder as he opened his eyes. He smiled at her and asked for help to his feet. Andie knew they had to get to safety, she wrapped her arm around his back, supporting him as they started walking back to the troops.

After a moment, Jonathan looked deep in her eyes and asked, "What took you so long to figure that out?"

"I reacted before I thought about what I was doing," she admitted. At that moment, she realized she could have prevented him from being injured in the first place. If she had acted in the manner King had instructed her, the beast would never have gone so far. Andie could have put the beast on the run from the beginning.

"This isn't going to happen again, I promise," Andie determined with all her heart. The confrontation with the beast made her realize that she had to completely absorb and execute every instruction she had been given. Total surrender to her King was vital for her to be able to fulfill her mission.

The troops cheered for the two warriors when they returned to the safety of camp. Immediately, Jonathan was given clean clothes, fresh water to drink, and his wound was dressed.

Andie felt she had screwed up and couldn't bring herself to look at King when he came to her. The warmth from his touch filled her with joy and sorrow at the same time. She began to cry, thinking she had failed to keep Jonathan safe from harm.

"Andie, why are you so upset? You have recovered your loved one," King asked, looking deep into her eyes. Her heart broke.

"I realize now I didn't do things right and he was injured because I was scared," she confessed, dropping her head.

King lifted her head to look into her eyes again, and said, "True, he was hurt, but you have learned a valuable lesson. Trusting in me and what you've been taught is the first lesson. After this, you'll be better equipped to handle the enemy.

You now have the Garnet stone of healing. You've learned how to use words in my authority to restore Life." A beautiful, deep red stone settled into place next to the others on her sword. His smile made her fears and worries melt away. She could feel her heart lighten as her mind cleared. She smiled as the breeze tousled her hair.

"I want to thank you, Andie, that was one of the scariest things I've ever been through," Jonathan professed.

"It was pretty scary for me too. I'm just so freakin' glad that you're ok." she gushed, pulling him close and hugging him tightly.

"I knew I would be ok, I trust my King completely, and I knew you wouldn't fail to stop that nasty thing, but it TOOK you long enough!" he laughed, pulling back from the hug.

"Fine, you just wait and see what happens next time." Andie responded, playfully punching his shoulder.

"We are all waiting for 'the next time'," said one of the soldiers, Emer. He had startling green eyes and that 'boy next door' look, despite being a seasoned warrior. He took this time to introduce her to the other soldiers in the fighting squad.

Ruben, with a long mop of brick red hair, and most comfortable swinging a battle axe, nodded in acknowledgement when described as gregarious and quick to volunteer for anything.

Aimon, who looked the youngest, was fair skinned, slender, with blue eyes and blond, spiked hair. He had the most tranquil voice she ever heard.

Next, dark skinned and towering over the group with his hands constantly rolled into fists was Thyst. A hit from him was like an assault from a war hammer.

Phire was the most laid back of the group. Having a lion's mane of bronze-brown hair, and biceps that resembled exploding cantaloupes, he nodded as he placed his hand over his heart. Andie learned that his reflexes were practically invisible to the eye.

Each one dipped his head with their introduction. She knew beyond a shadow of a doubt these soldiers were completely faithful and loyal to their King and would never hesitate to act on his orders. What bothered Andie was, they would listen to her as well.

King sensed something bothering Andie and asked her what she was thinking.

"I've read the account of the sacrifice. It really messed with my head, and I can't get the thought of all that torment out of my mind," Andie offered, "but I've been with you for a while now, and I haven't seen any scars like those described in the story. I'm not trying to be disrespectful, but could you show me?"

A hush fell over the garden. Even the breeze stilled. Slowly, King pulled his shirt over his head and opened his arms wide. The entire army of soldiers and warriors slowly dropped to one knee.

At first, Andie didn't see anything out of the ordinary, then she noticed long, red streaks across his chest and arms. He turned around slowly so she could see his back and as she watched, hideous bloody gouges emerged on his flesh. As he kept turning, they continued to grow and deepen in color. Andie thought she saw him flinch when one particularly horrible scar rose across his forehead. From what she had read, a repulsive circle of thorns had been ground into the flesh of his head. The enemy took great delight in torturing King and ripped chunks of flesh from his body with every blow from the massive weapons of hate and humiliation. There wasn't an inch of him that wasn't bloodied with the scars of excruciating torture.

Just when she thought she couldn't look anymore, she noticed even his hands and feet had been torn open, and ghastly rope burns circled his neck. In addition to all the beatings, torture, and shame, he was hung from a tree for all to watch him slowly die.

The soldiers didn't understand why their King had allowed this to happen. They were sure he knew the enemy wouldn't stop tormenting the people they were trying to rescue. But he was the King, and the soldiers waited anxiously for the slightest whisper of a command from him.

None came.

Tears fell from his eyes, streaming down his cheeks as he looked Andie in the eye, and said, "I love you, so very much."

When the realization of the sacrifice hit Andie, she went weak and fell to her knees, sobbing from the depths of her heart. This was the treatment that was in store for everyone who didn't return to the King. But, because of his willingness to go through that torment for their sake, they wouldn't *have* to endure the pain or be separated from the one person who loves them more than anyone else. They only had to accept this gift of love from him, and once again live in their true home.

King pulled his shirt on and helped Andie to her feet. He held her in a tender embrace. The rest of the soldiers stood as well. The breeze stirred again. As the scars slowly faded, they were forever etched in her heart as the price he paid for her.

Emer stepped forward and said, "We simply cannot fathom the depth of compassion he has for the lost ones. We hold the highest respect for our King and his sacrifice. We've been with him from before the beginning of Time, and we are constantly amazed at how his loved ones can move him to tears or cause him the greatest joy. If everyone knew how tenderhearted he was, we believe all would return. But, as he said, the lost ones have been blinded by the enemy."

Aimon joined Emer saying, "Andie, we are willing to do whatever it takes to help you in recovering the lost ones. The whole kingdom rejoices when he is moved to joy, and that causes us to become stronger in our mission to help find them all. We can't do this without you. Please, allow us to be a part of bringing joy to the King like so many of his loved ones have done."

Andie studied the soldiers. They watched King's every movement as he moved through the camp. She couldn't understand how so many people could care about each other in such a wonderful way. They were as devoted to their King as he was to his lost loved ones. The look on his face was one of pure delight as he spoke of his loved ones. "*That must be what it's like to be in love,*" Andie thought. "*If I could just feel what they feel...*"

Once again, she jumped when he spoke to her, "My love is obsessive, immeasurable, and overflowing for my loved ones—that includes you, Andie. I have been calling you, pursuing you longer than you will ever know. I wouldn't rest until I had your attention. I have poured out my heart for you, my beloved. You've seen a small part of my heart in the wondrous creations I made for you, but you have no idea how much *I desire, I long, to be a part of your life.* I was crushed when you ignored me. Those moments were more painful than the torture of the sacrifice. The enemy could never hurt me as badly as my own loved ones when they refuse to hear or return to me. Worse than all the pain I've gone through, is the hurt it causes my Father."

"*His Father?*" Now Andie felt like there was more going on than she was aware of, and began to ask a question...

"Yes Andie, my Father is the one who set me up as King in Covenant, over all creation. And out of my heart for him, I knew we had to find a way to bring the loved ones home again. That is how we came up with the sacrifice. The enemy was so self-absorbed, he never realized that my exchange was for the total release of all the lost ones. Afterwards, that evil incarnate figured out what happened and put his full force behind deceiving the lost ones."

"Can I take a time out? There is too much going on here for me to wrap my head around," she was torn between staying and finding out more from King, but she wanted to get a handle on things before he went further. After the realization of the sacrifice hitting her heart so hard, and now, there is another person involved, she wanted to process things, quietly.

"I thought you would want some time alone, but don't let your guard down, the enemy is still out there. I don't want anything to happen to you," he stated, then turned and whispered to Emer. Andie was quite sure it was none of her business what he was saying to Emer, so she turned and walked away.

"*Ok, now, we have a King who has been calling me his beloved. The same person who allowed himself to go through unimaginable pain, torture, and death for me and those he calls his lost ones. He had soldiers already lined up and ready to fight with me to find the other lost ones, and now he is talking about his Father. This couldn't get more confusing if he tried!*" Andie's thoughts tumbled through her mind as she wandered through the trees. She began to realize that there weren't any weeds or thorn bushes in this garden, just beauty, peace, a cool breeze, and soldiers who look like they've been sculpted from a solid slab of marble.

Yes, they were musclebound, but for some reason, Andie didn't feel attracted to them as she would have if she had seen them in school. Heaven forbid! There would have been rampant pandemonium among the students if *they* had shown up at her school. The boys would have been intimidated, feeling challenged and the hormone-charged girls would have them hiding in a bathroom. She giggled. The thought of these battle-hardened soldiers running from a bunch of girls was just what she needed to lighten her mood.

Watching them from a distance, she began to imagine what they would look like if they were to show up in her school world.

Phire, with his wild mane of hair would be comfortable in a sleeveless denim shirt showing off his tanned biceps, wearing jeans and motorcycle boots. Probably riding a motorcycle. Yep, definitely riding a motorcycle.

Thyst, with his ebony skin, was more likely to wear a deep purple long sleeve shirt, dark slacks, and dress shoes. Wait, turn up the cuffs on the sleeves, gotta leave room for his incredible reach with those lightning-fast fists.

Aimon, looking like the youngest of the group, would be perfectly happy in a white t-shirt, black jeans, and Converse tennis shoes, riding a skateboard.

Emer, who never left her side unless asked by King, would most likely be wearing a green shirt, khaki shorts, and sneakers. He had a curl of dark hair that would never stay in place.

Then there was Ruben. This dude was straight from Middle Earth, with his long red hair pulled back from his face in a loose braid. If any one of them would have a beard, it would be Ruben. Do you need a volunteer to fell a tree, chase down wild animals, jump off a cliff? -he's your guy. He was no fool, just ready for whatever needed to be done.

Watching them, she smiled to herself. She felt honored to have been taught to fight with the likes of those soldiers. She hoped she could become a leader they could respect.

Chapter 6

New Plans

While walking through this spectacular paradise, and without realizing it, she had walked upon a gentleman sitting under a tree who was enjoying the breeze with his eyes closed. It startled her more than him. She quickly apologized for intruding, but he dismissed the apology with a wave and invited her to visit for a while. Andie couldn't tell if it was just this place, or if it was this person, but she knew she was completely safe and sat down under the green canopy of the magnificent tree.

He didn't look directly at her, but instead asked her what she thought of the garden. Andie just soaked up the coolness in the breeze, breathed in the fragrance in the air, and thought to herself how wonderful it felt to be here. Once again, calling this her real home.

"Wonderful, that's exactly what I wanted you to feel, dearest. This IS your true home and I'm so glad we can spend time here now," he shared.

"*Yikes, he can hear my thoughts....*" she stopped as the realization slammed into her thoughts, he was the Father. "*Geesh, this just keeps getting better...*" She smiled, and he smiled in return.

Andie couldn't figure out why, but with the breeze blowing through her hair and a gentle coolness washing over her, she started to giggle. Although she tried to be quiet, she couldn't help herself. It dawned on her that he was laughing as well. "What is the deal?" she asked.

He looked at her. Her heart banged in her chest as their eyes met. He was the embodiment of Love itself and she felt electricity course through her body, erupting into laughter.

Without a second's hesitation, she threw her arms around his neck and was laughing and crying at the same time. He wrapped his arms around her gently, and yet so completely encompassing. They held onto each other for what felt like an eternity and couldn't bring themselves to let go. Andie's emotions were going haywire, and she couldn't tell 'up' from 'down.' She couldn't make sense of it all.

Ecstatic joy overwhelmed her, and she had a glimpse into what she could only describe as the heart of the Father. Now, she understood *why* the King did *what* he did for the loved ones. Her heart began to break, all the torment she had gone through in all the years before this moment in time simply dissolved as she felt his love fully encompass her.

Andie pulled away to sit back down and realized he would never have let go if she hadn't moved first, and that would have been fine with her. It was then she saw Emer standing off to the side with a smile on his face. His hand was on his heart. She then remembered how much they cared for the King and the Father. They sat in silence for several long minutes with their arms linked. She couldn't let go of him. He didn't show any signs of wanting to let go either. Together they enjoyed the fragrance of the flowering trees; and the beautiful colors that sprang up from the earth in bursts of red, pink, and green caressing their every view.

The trees gently swayed with the breeze and shared their whispers as the Father and Andie enjoyed the cool of the evening, safe in the arms of someone they loved and couldn't bear the thought of leaving. Time seemed to stop when he looked into her eyes, she knew there was nobody else who could make her laugh and cause her spirit to soar like this person.

He spoke to her for just a few moments. But to her it was a lifetime, and she knew she *would never, could never* be away from him for too long. No sooner had the thought of leaving come to her mind that she felt a twinge of sadness creep into her chest. One more look into his eyes and her fears vanished. Leaning against him, she relaxed beyond imagination. And smiled.

-... .-.. --- --- -..

Without warning, a battle cry was heard, and the troops fell into formation awaiting instructions. The beast was back with hundreds more.

Andie felt her heart jump into her throat. "Oh my God, what are we going to do?" she whispered.

"We're going to destroy them," was the reply. "Andie, we're waiting, give the orders..." Emer suggested, rather strongly as they joined the rest of the soldiers.

She fumbled, not sure what orders she was supposed to give. "Destroy them!" she yelled.

The battle group ran in formation with her, flanking her on all sides. Phire ran in front and just to the left of her while Thyst stationed to the right front. Aimon stayed at her left side with Emer so close, he was almost touching her right elbow. Ruben brought up the rear, constantly surveying the surroundings.

Andie wasn't sure if she was awake or dreaming as she ran into the fray. "*This can't be happening,*" she whispered.

Emer was so close to her that he heard her comment, and spoke up, "You have to believe in what we're doing, or we'll lose this battle." The look in his eyes told her that this was as serious, and as real as the battle she had experienced before with Jonathan's capture.

"*Andie, remember I'm as close as your heartbeat.*" These words were all the reassurance she needed. She swung her sword hard as the sound of metal slamming against metal filled the air. Multitudes of metallic collisions exploded across the battlefield.

Horrific, guttural screeching burst from the throats of the demonic beasts. Ear splitting wails of pain and misery exploded from every side with an array of blood splattering the air and ground as they ran. Just as she thought she saw a sword coming toward her, Ruben deflected the blow and struck down the next monster in line.

Every swing of Andie's weapon built her courage and hardened her resolve. Seeing her troops fighting the enemy and defending her as well, made it clear they weren't going to give up for anything. She was determined she wasn't going to back down.

Andie wasn't sure if the next thing she heard was imagined or real. The voice was firm but gentle. "Andie, remember your training... we can use our swords, but you can use your words to stop these beasts from advancing," Aimon spoke into her ear as Thyst slammed his massive fist into the face of a beast.

Courage swept over her, and she spoke as loudly as she could, "Demons of Hate, STOP NOW! I COMMAND YOU, IN THE AUTHORITY OF THE KING, TO LEAVE!"

A surge of relief flooded her heart as the beasts stopped advancing and some even turned away, still shrieking. Ruben took up the chase after one came dangerously close to her.

She never saw the blow from behind that slammed into her body.

Her world tilted, blurred, and faded into blackness.

"NOOOOOO!!!" Emer screamed, dropping to his knees.

Andie was injured so badly that she finally begged for relief. Her body slumped, Emer held her head in his lap.

A peace and calmness that can't be described washed over her. She realized she could still hear and was conscious of her surroundings, but pain was absent.

"*Ha, incredible...*" was her first thought. "*Wait, What? What do I do now?*" was her second thought.

Then came the realization that she had died. But, she hadn't 'disappeared.' She was still very much 'there.' It reminded her of the first time she stepped into Covenant Garden. She no longer felt pain, just relief. She could hear the wind rushing around her, but she couldn't feel it on her skin. Andie thought, "*This can't be over now, there is still so much more I have to do. Now I know that no matter what happens to me, I will always be alive.*"

"*Use your words....*"

Suddenly, the pain was back, causing her to suck in great volumes of air, and she commanded the pain to stop. As she opened her eyes, that is exactly what she did. Barely speaking above a whisper, "Pain, you will leave; Body, be restored! I am a warrior of the King and I speak in HIS AUTHORITY! " Andie was caught by surprise but pleased at how her body began to respond to her words.

At once, the familiar peace that comes with the rushing wind blew through her spirit and body causing her to gasp out loud again. It was as if He stepped into her body, strengthened her arms, calmed her heart, and built up her courage. She understood now he would always be closer than her heartbeat. Andie realized that if she obeyed his commands, she could do anything he asked of her. He was the strength, peace, and courage that she needed. A total serenity engulfed her and at the same time energized her into action.

"Oh, NOTHING can stop me now!" she said to nobody in particular as Emer helped her to her feet and they ran to join the rest of the troops. Little did she know that all the kingdom heard her words, as well as the dark dominion of the enemy.

-... .-.. --- --- -..

"Now we have to expose a weak spot that she won't expect," surmised an evil incarnate.

The battle had subsided as the troops accompanied Andie back to camp, relating their story to King. He held her in his arms and as she rested in his embrace, the feeling of cool water rushing through her body was refreshing, strengthening, and something she never wanted to end.

She wasn't sure why, but there was a sneaky smile crawling across the King's face as he said, "I've decided to let

Ruben join you on the other side." Stunned was the reaction on everyone's face except for King and the Father.

"Okay, uh, why?" was Andie's response. Right away Ruben's eyes opened wide in shock, nobody had ever questioned King, so this was new.

All heads swiveled to watch King as he responded, "I think it's time for him to have a better understanding of your world, in your own shoes and not just as a messenger for me. And I think there is a good deal you could learn from him as well."

Once again, the heads swiveled back to Andie, "Okay, but there is no way he could go to school with me, there are rules, you know," she stated, matter-of-factly.

Back to King, for the game point, "He will stay at Katie's house as Katie's cousin. You need to learn how literally he takes things and just how powerful your words are in every situation."

Andie had grown fond of these soldiers, and couldn't help but think that Ruben would find it difficult to blend in. Maybe that was the point. Whatever the point was, this was going to be interesting, no matter how you looked at it. A smile passed between the Father and King. Ruben was smiling. Andie giggled, whether from nervousness or amusement, she couldn't tell.

Katie took the news of the house guest with pleasure. She let him get settled into one of the spare rooms near Andie's room. The two of them chatted like old friends catching up over coffee.

Katie had allowed Jonathan to invite his best friend Donovan over for a sleepover with movies and video games before the holiday break was over. The boys had been best friends since the time when Donovan punched Jonathan in the nose and Jonathan punched him back. Foolproof formula for best friends!

"That works," Andie thought. She needed time to figure out what to do now that she had been to this glorious paradise, but Christmas break would be over soon, and she would have to go back to school. *"What a bummer..."*

Chapter 7

New Friends

The first couple of days of school weren't too bad. Most of the same faces, but she felt differently about them now. Andie constantly thought about King. There were times when she caught herself daydreaming about Covenant Garden, but surprisingly, didn't miss a beat as far as classes were concerned. She felt energized when her thoughts wandered off. This in turn, brought focus and clarity to her studies. Ideas for projects jumped onto the pages of her notebook. Boring book reports took on new life as she sailed through the reading. Occasionally, she thought she recognized a familiar white t-shirt and black jeans passing her in the hallways.

At first, Andie wasn't sure if she would like to have another guy around the house, but Ruben settled in quickly and took over some of the chores. After having some of Katie's brownies, he was hooked on chocolate. There were things about Ruben that Andie hadn't noticed in the beginning. For instance, he could just appear from nowhere, moving soundlessly. He would spend time by himself in the morning, walking through the garden in the back of the house. Andie was sure she heard him talking to himself, but she didn't want to intrude. Ruben liked to whistle while we went around the house. Something about the tune reminded Andie of when she heard the birds in Covenant Garden. She missed spending time there, but with schoolwork piling up, she hadn't spent a lot of time with King.

One day, there was a new student in her class. This girl was the polar opposite of Andie. Perky and with a figure that drove the boys crazy, lydee (*all lowercase because she said, "it looks sooo cute when you write out!"*) seemed to ride the wave of adoration with pleasure.

Andie saw trouble and couldn't get over the way everyone fawned over her. What really bugged Andie was, even though lydee had the attention of the entire student body, she wouldn't stay away from Andie. Everywhere she went, lydee insisted on trying to talk to her, to be her best friend, inviting her to parties, pushing her way into everything Andie tried to do.

She spent more time dealing with lydee than anything else, and she couldn't figure out why this girl went out of her way to get her attention when she had the attention of hundreds of others clamoring to be a part of her world. Whatever the reason, Andie was getting tired of the constant badgering.

Andie couldn't really put her finger on what bothered her about lydee and even began to think that maybe this could be a test to see how she would react in a 'real world' application of Kings' love for the lost ones. So, for no other reason but to get her to back off, Andie invited lydee to dinner. Andie talked to Katie about asking lydee over and Katie agreed. It never occurred to Andie to mention this to Ruben.

Andie had lydee come over after school on Friday and the girls offered to make dinner. Spaghetti should be easy enough. Jonathan sneaked in and snagged a brownie before heading up to his room and doing homework. "Who's that?" lydee asked, watching him climb the stairs.

"That's Jonathan, my cousin." Andie stated as she watched lydee watching him, "He's too young for you."

"Good grief, I just wanted to know who he was. Relax!" lydee shot back, grabbing the spoon to stir the sauce. *"But it's good to know who I'm dealing with..."*

Katie set the table and thanked the girls for cooking supper as they all sat down to eat. Katie said a blessing over the food and noticed lydee squirmed a bit but hadn't thought to ask if her family said a blessing or not. "*Well, 'be a witness' to everyone,*" she thought to herself.

"So, 'lydee,' that's such an unusual name. Where did it come from?" Katie asked, passing the pasta.

"I was named after my father's middle name, Lyric Dean. I like to keep the 'L' lowercase because it's just cuter that way when I write it," lydee explained, passing the pasta to Andie.

"That's fun, so what does your father do for a living?" Katie was trying to get to know a little more about Andie's newest friend, someone who has been a constant part of Andie's life the past few weeks. Katie was happy for Andie to have friends again.

"My father is in corporate takeovers of weak and failing companies. Gosh, that sounds harsh, he actually offers what they want as long as they come under his control," lydee explained, rather rehearsed.

"Well, I guess as long as he can help people out, that's good," Katie responded, beginning to wonder what seasoning they used when cooking. Her stomach was a little unsettled. Looking down at her plate, she asked, "So, have you been cooking very long, lydee?"

"Ha!" she laughed, "no way! The servants do that at home, I just thought it would be fun to try it out here. I hope that's ok with you…" Looking at Katie, a strange expression crept across lydee's face, almost smiling at Katie's discomfort.

"No, that's ok, I was just wondering," Katie replied, sipping her drink, and continued, "What does your mother do?"

"She's dead and I do not like to talk about it," shutting off that line of questioning quickly, lydee stone cold stared at Katie with her own question, "Where's your husband?"

Jonathan froze. Taken aback as if slapped in the face, Katie had to gather her senses and firmly replied, "He's been dead for a few years as well, and I know how uncomfortable it is to talk about, so I apologize for hurting your feelings."

"Oh no, I didn't mean to be rude," lydee's voice was hollow and had a slight edge. Both Andie and Katie took note not to ask about that again. Jonathan silently mouthed, "*WOW!*"

"There's a great sale going on downtown tomorrow, Andie we have to go!" lydee was suddenly a cheerful party girl again, reaching for Andie's hand, "I want to treat you to a shopping spree, come on, say we can go!" Looking at Katie, lydee put on those pouty puppy dog eyes that nobody can resist.

"Of course, you should go," Katie searched Andie's face. It was obvious, she really wanted to go shopping, and if lydee was offering, why not?

Imagine the surprise on Katie's face when, while they were talking over dinner, Ruben walked in, skidded to a stop, and stared at the back of lydee's head while instinctively balling his fists. His face went red as he backed out of the room. Katie excused herself and went to find Ruben. He was in the garden, pacing the walkway, talking under his breath. Katie sensed that he wasn't happy with their dinner companion.

"Do you realize who that is at your table?" was all he could say.

Katie closed her eyes and realized the "knot" in her stomach that suddenly appeared when lydee entered the house was a sign she somehow overlooked in her effort to help Andie entertain her new friend.

-... .-.. --- --- -..

A battalion of soldiers mustered, awaiting orders, ready for the fight that lay ahead.

-... .-.. --- --- -..

Taking advantage of Katie's absence, lydee invited Andie to her house for a sleepover with a few other friends. Feeling a growing acceptance from the most popular girl in school, Andie accepted the invitation. A weight dropped in her heart. She really needed to get back to Covenant and spend time with King, but she didn't want to miss out on her chance to be a part of something she never had experienced before– the IN crowd. Pushing the feeling aside, she went to find Katie and ask permission to sleep over. Jonathan stared in disbelief, still shaken from the conversation, and excused himself from the table.

Permission was granted and the sleepover went off without a hitch. Andie met several girls that she recognized from school but had never spoken to her. Everyone seemed nice, and Andie couldn't remember having this much fun before.

The next couple of weeks flew by with Andie and lydee spending every moment together studying, shopping, and partying. Andie hadn't even heard of some of the fabulous stores they visited. The girls always came home with several bags overflowing with wonderful new clothes, makeup, shoes, and jewelry.

Andie teased lydee, "Most of the stores would go bankrupt if it weren't for you!" That simply made lydee want to go to the mall again. Occasionally, it would be a group trip with several girls hitting the shops, eating, going to the movies or sometimes, sneaking into clubs with fake id's lydee had made for them. lydee always seemed to have money to spend on anything she wanted. Mystery surrounded lydee. Quite frankly, it scared Andie, but she was enjoying the attention from the new set of friends in her life.

Just as Andie started to think that spending so much time with lydee might not be such a good thing, she met Kevin. He was so cute. And when she linked arms with him, she could feel the strength in his. For a moment, she remembered King's arms, but Kevin distracted her with a quick kiss. Oh, those kisses. Andie had never dreamed of what a kiss could do to her, and Kevin's kisses made her knees go weak. So, of course, he had to hold her close to keep her from falling. Kevin doted on Andie in such a way that, even when she was briefly away from him, she missed his responsiveness. Having spent a good deal of her life feeling very invisible, she desperately craved the attention.

Katie asked Andie, "Honey, when was the last time you talked with King? Don't you think you should make some time to get back in touch with your mission?"

Ruben spoke to her for the first time in days, "Andie, King has been asking about you and when you might return, we only have a short time before it will be too late."

"Oh my God!" Andie screamed, "I can't believe you want me to give up all the things you KNOW I've wanted all my life!" Her heart slammed in her chest as if it would explode. Something nagged at the back of her mind, she had never spoken to Katie that way before and part of her brain tried to figure out what the heck was going on.

Her phone rang up lydee's ringtone. Answering it and leaving the room quickly, Andie said, "Hey, what's up?"

Ruben and Katie exchanged a shocked look, Jonathan sat stunned at Andie's outburst.

-... .-.. --- --- -..

The battlefield was strewn with the carcasses of final attempts of deceptions, betrayals, and the promises of hope. It was a bloody mess and exhausting for those in the throes of battle, but their King wouldn't retreat, he was fighting for his love.

Chapter 8

Falling Deeper

"Hey girl, our favorite band is playing at the club tonight, and we're going. Get your stuff together. I'll be over in a minute to pick you up!" lydee ordered.

Looking back at Katie and Ruben, Andie's heart wrestled with her decision, but she had to stand up for what she wanted, or she would lose it all. Kevin might even break up with her and she wasn't about to lose another guy. She went upstairs to get her things.

"That's it, I'll be back later," Ruben growled, stomping off towards the library. Katie fought back the tears welling up. Jonathan wrapped his arms around his mom.

Andie hopped into the car, and lydee demanded a quick shopping trip, "I hope you don't plan on wearing that getup. We'll get some clothes and hit the club. I hear the band is on fire tonight!"

Once again, lydee dressed Andie in amazing clothes she never would have picked out for herself. She had to admit, she looked awesome.

As foretold, the band was incredible. As the music pulsed, the drinks poured like a gushing river. Andie tried to stay out of the 'hard stuff' but couldn't always keep lydee from pouring something into her drink. As a result of the alcohol lydee was able to sneak in her drinks, Andie lost her inhibitions, broke character, and cleared the dance floor with her astounding dance moves. She had never felt so alive, so invincible, and so dangerous. She wanted to kiss a strange guy just to see what it felt like.

Part of her mind—the not-so-fuzzy part—tried to warn her, but she had become quite good at dismissing those nagging little thoughts. Andie grabbed the smokin' hot dude that had been watching her all night and kissed him hard.

However, when she tried to pull away, he wouldn't let her go. He had a grip that was so tight, she thought he would break her arm. Andie tried to push him away, screaming for lydee to help her. lydee nevertheless, kept dancing. Watching with a sinister grin, she relished the scene. The guy grabbed Andie close to kiss her again. This time his hot alcohol breath gagged her.

She struggled, screaming, "HELP ME! HELP!" All the eyes that looked in her direction were black, soulless portals.

Once again, the guy pressed himself against her body and thoroughly enjoyed watching her fight back. Everyone in the room ignored her. She felt trapped in a soundproof bubble. With one arm wrapped around her, he used his other hand to yank her hair back, licking her throat from the base of her neck up to her ear, he whispered, "I won't let you go until I get everything I want from you, sugar." Time crawled through mud. She could hear her heartbeat in her ears. Her body raged with heat and anger. Her voice raspy from screaming and she could barely catch her breath.

Fear gripped Andie like an iron straight jacket. More than once, she thought she would pass out. Everything went blurry a couple of times. Knowing that giving up would be a mistake, she fought to stay awake. The more she struggled against his grip, the more he laughed and yanked her close. Several times, he kissed her mouth so hard she nearly suffocated. Pulling on her shirt, he licked his lips like a hungry animal. He kept loosening his grip enough to let her think she could escape, just to force her body against his again. lydee laughed, gyrating with a cluster of guys, always making sure Andie could see she was watching her struggle. The more Andie screamed and fought back, the more lydee reveled in her terror.

The guy started making his way to the door with Andie still pressed against him. She panicked, knowing what would happen if they left. She was crying and trying to fight back, but to no avail. Andie screamed, "OH MY GOD, HELP ME!!" From somewhere in the ether, in a blur of motion, an iron fist flew into the guys' face, sending him reeling into the bar with Andie still in his grip. She landed on top of him, but he was out cold.

Another set of strong hands grabbed Andie's shoulders and pulled her up to her feet. She had already decided that she would kill someone if needed. Kevin finally reached her–he turned her around and held her close. Andie fell into his embrace crying, trying to keep up with him as they stepped over the body of the guy who had tormented her.

"Where is lydee?" Kevin asked. The mention of her name made Andie want to vomit.

"I don't care, she watched that brute do all that crap to me and never tried to help me!" she screamed.

Then, she did throw up.

As Kevin drove her home, he called Katie to let her know what happened. Andie cried continually and expected all hell to break loose when she got home. But there was no screaming, blaming, or accusations. Ruben carried her to her room. Jonathan thanked Kevin for bringing her home and closed the door after him. Katie helped her change clothes and cleaned up a little before she passed out in her bed. Ruben held Katie in a tight hug, and suggested she spend time with King. He would watch out for everyone at the house. Jonathan joined Katie as she headed to the library.

Ruben whistled as he geared up for what might be a long night and he was secretly ready for battle He banged his fist against his chest and quietly sounded a battle cry. He didn't want to give away his position.

-... .-.. --- --- -..

King, breathing hard and sweating profusely, stopped fighting to wipe his brow, and whispered a soft prayer of gratitude to the Father for the end of that battle. Several soldiers gathered around him, offering assistance with water, and a place to rest.

-... .-.. --- --- -..

Andie spent most of the next day in bed before she tried to get up and shower. Her stomach still flip-flopped around, constantly threatening a repeat performance. The slightest noise made her head almost explode, but she had to go to the bathroom before she wet the bed. She felt like death warmed up, scrambled, thrown into the sink disposal, and chucked back out. And that was *after* she began to feel better. Her eyes burned, her head swam, and her fingernails felt like they were on too tight.

Katie opened the bathroom door a little and said, "Andie, I'll change the sheets while you shower and get medicine to settle your stomach." Closing the door carefully, she fought back the lump in her throat. Katie had been so worried while Andie was gone, that she simply couldn't focus on anything else, so she tried to clean the house. Katie hadn't felt this helpless in so long and it startled her when Ruben spoke.

"Is she feeling any better?" he asked. Ruben was back to his old self. Ready for anyone, anything, anywhere.

Andie expected to be in so much trouble when she finally descended the stairs. Instead, Katie and Ruben carried on their conversation, as if nothing had happened. Katie did mention that lydee had called several times, but she turned off Andie's phone so she could sleep. Andie never wanted to see that little witch again. Thankful to be home and with the people she loved, she slowly eased back into the familiar routine of home.

Returning to school after a three-day weekend, Andie tried to avoid lydee as much as possible. She didn't want to talk with anyone. And that is exactly what happened. People watched her walk by, whispering and giggling when she looked at them.

Kevin joined her in the hallway, sensing she was out of sorts and asked, "What's the matter, Andie, you seem just as upset today as you did the other night."

"Kevin, do you notice anything different about the way people are acting toward me?" she pointed out.

"That could be because lydee made it sound like you did things 'good girls' shouldn't," he replied innocently.

"WHAT?!" Andie screeched, trying to keep her voice down. "That little witch watched what happened and enjoyed it, she never tried to help me!" A familiar taste crept up the back of her throat. A guy in a green T-shirt, trying to get past them, bumped Andie's arm. She regained control of her emotions.

"Hey girl, whatcha doing?" A familiar, yet sickening voice reached Andie's ears.

Andie reeled around and wanted to beat the living crap out of this spiteful excuse for a human. "I could kill you for letting that guy hurt me, and you didn't even TRY to help!" Andie blurted.

Anger flashed red in lydee's eyes, then turned to mock concern as she replied, "Oh honey, I was so wasted I didn't know what was happening until Kevin told me the next day. I was so worried about you and wanted to come over. I kept calling but you wouldn't answer, so I thought for sure that you hated me. I've been so lonely without my best friend." lydee put on her fake pouty face just to put it over the top. "Please, don't hurt me anymore by pushing me away. I only wanted to have a good time with my bestie, but you started putting the moves on that guy and I was afraid you would hurt Kevin." (pause for effect) "I just can't remember much of what happened. I was so hurt. I couldn't believe my best friend would do something like that to me," lydee reached for Andie's hand, grasping it so hard it began to hurt. Andie snatched it away, causing lydee to whimper and pout again.

"Don't be like that, Andie, she's upset." Kevin naively reacted.

"Are you kidding me!" Andie shouted, "She's trying to make it sound like I'M the one who messed things up!" Her stomach reminded her to settle down, or things would get ugly again.

Kevin hugged lydee and apologized for Andie. lydee watched Andie with the same sinister smile she wore at the club, "I'm sure Andie will come around in a couple of days and things will get back to normal," he reassured lydee. Things hadn't been 'normal' since the day Andie invited lydee over for supper.

-... .-.. --- --- -..

King sat by himself, looking out over the valley and watched the battle raging below.

-... .-.. --- --- -..

After several days of schoolwork, doing chores, and trying to forget the most humiliating night of her life, Andie began to feel better about things. She had only talked to Kevin a couple of times, and really missed him. She even began to feel bad for screaming at lydee and decided to call her. After a couple of rings, lydee picked up.

Andie asked, "Hi lydee, how are you?" and continued with, "I'm really sorry for the way I acted the other day, I was scared, sick, and confused."

It was longer than Andie would have liked to wait before lydee answered, "I know, I've missed my bestie. Wanna go get something to eat? My treat!" No big surprise there.

"Sure, in 30 minutes?" Andie replied.

"I'll be there in ten, bye!" lydee responded.

Now, to tell Katie that she was going out.

Andie was surprised to find that Kevin and Jonathan were at the same fast-food place near the high school. They were talking over their food and looked up when lydee made an entrance.

"Hey Kevin, look, I have your sweetie pie here for you!" lydee announced as she threw the door open, looking at all the patrons. People always stopped to watch her. It was like passing a car wreck—you know you shouldn't look, but you just can't resist.

"lydee, stop. You're embarrassing him," Andie interjected, smiling as she slid into the booth next to Kevin.

lydee had already sat down next to Jonathan. Real close. Uncomfortably close. As Jonathan tried to scoot a little bit farther away by putting his jacket between them, Andie reminded lydee they needed to order. Handing over her credit card, lydee said, "Surprise me!" and bounced off to the bathroom with her far-too-short mini skirt flashing too much skin. A flicker of a thought crossed her mind, but Andie dismissed it. After all, she WAS trying to make amends with lydee.

Upon lydee's return, Kevin offered, "Hey Andie, did lydee tell you about the party this weekend? It's at the Baker twins' house and their parents will be out of town, but their uncle will be there." What he didn't mention was the uncle was only a couple of years older than the Baker twins.

"I absolutely insist that Jonathan come with us!" lydee demanded. Jonathan nervously looked at Andie and replied, "We can't. We're having dinner with some long-time friends of ours, the Aldrich's, Donovan's family."

Andie thought about it for a second and answered, "I think we could get away after supper for a little bit. We'll have to see," hoping that would satisfy lydee. Glancing at Jonathan, hoping that would satisfy him as well.

"No more arguing, you guys WILL come, I'll pick you up!" lydee demanded, then flashed her fake smile and winked. All three friends sat there looking at her and this new, demanding facet of her personality. Andie looked at Jonathan as he mouthed the words, "*No way...*"

"Jonathan, sweetie, let me wear your jacket, it's so cold in here," lydee ordered, as she slipped her arms into his favorite jacket. Getting up to leave, she told Andie, "Let's go find our outfits for the party. We're gonna *kill* with how good we're gonna look!" She leaned over the table and flashed her cleavage at Jonathan as she kissed him on the cheek. Poor Jonathan sat there, stunned, blushing, and more than just a little upset with lydee.

It's amazing how fast life can change in the span of thirty minutes.

Chapter 9

Life of the Party

True to her word, lydee spent tons of money with Andie shopping, having fun with her 'bestie' again. Andie was happy to be having fun again, but a part of her wanted to make darn sure there wouldn't be a repeat performance of the club fiasco.

"Andie, you really should wear this adorable little skirt instead of those pants. Dang, you look so old!" lydee whined, shoving her hands into the pockets of Jonathan's jacket she was wearing.

"No, lydee, get over it. I'm wearing the pants and you can wear the skirt or whatever. I want to look nice, but there is no need to draw unnecessary attention to ourselves.

lydee was taken aback by Andie's boldness, so she tried to run things around to her favor again. "Fine, let's go look at the jewelry..."

No matter how hard she tried, Andie couldn't shake the feeling that she really should cancel going to the party. As if she could read Andie's mind, lydee always managed to distract Andie with something else. Nothing could have prepared Andie for lydee's next suggestion.

Looking dead into Andie's eyes, lydee inquired, "So, when are you and Kevin gonna, you know–hook up?" Andie could not believe what she was hearing. lydee continually acted like nothing had happened at the club. How could she even ask a question like that? What business was it of hers?

"What about you, lydee? Have you ever hooked up with someone?" Andie fired off. Without missing a beat, lydee went on saying, "At this one party, I was so drunk and wasted, I don't remember who he was, but I always get what I want." lydee's eyes burned straight into Andie's soul.

"Ahh, hit a nerve, did we?" Andie thought maybe lydee had a sore spot. But the hateful twisted look on lydee's face wasn't something Andie wanted to see again, so she skipped around the topic and suggested they get something to drink.

-... .-.. --- --- -..

Supper with Katie and Jonathan's friends, the Aldrich's, was a quiet affair. They had been Katie's church pastors and best friends. It was they who helped her recover from losing her husband, and that was about the same time Donovan and Jonathan became friends. They enjoyed casual talk about memories of past adventures and plans for the future. Jonathan kept looking at Andie nervously, then he motioned for her to meet him in the kitchen.

"Katie, we'll get the dishes," Andie offered, while she and Jonathan cleared the table.

"I am not going to that party, and I don't think you should either, Andie." Jonathan stated, setting plates in the sink, uncharacteristically demanding.

"Don't worry, Kevin will be there, and I won't let him leave my side. I've already called dibs on 'designated driver' because you know that will be a necessity with lydee around. I swear, I don't think she even has a liver," she joked, but Jonathan wasn't smiling. He simply looked at her, wishing he could get back the Andie he loved.

Andie took care of the leftover food while Jonathan loaded the dishwasher. She desperately hoped he wasn't too mad with her. He was the closest thing she had to having a brother.

Andie changed clothes and said her goodbyes with a quick kiss on Katie's cheek, and a shoulder hug for Jonathan seated at the table again. Katie and Jonathan exchanged silent glances, each knowing what the other felt.

Right on cue, lydee pulled up to the door, screeching tires, sending gravel flying across the driveway.

"I have my phone, so if anything happens, I'll call you," was Andie's (hopefully) reassuring comment as she closed the door behind her. Jonathan and Donovan exchanged glances and headed to the library to work on their model cars. Katie offered coffee to go with the ensuing small talk at the table.

Andie didn't hear much of lydee's chatter on the way to the party. An ache was growing in her chest. At times it felt as if her heart was breaking, almost as if she were connected to someone experiencing devastating trauma. When tears started the creep down her cheeks, lydee demanded to know why. All Andie could say was, "The dust in the air is killing my allergies," while carefully dabbing her eyes with a tissue so she didn't ruin her makeup.

-... .-.. --- --- -..

Tears rolled down King's cheek. Father closed his eyes and leaned against his tree.

-... .-.. --- --- -..

"Well, clean it up, 'cause we are going to paar-ty!" lydee ordered, swinging into the driveway of the Baker twins' house.

Kevin met the girls at the door, kissing Andie on the cheek. He took their jackets, and it was then that Andie noticed lydee had on Jonathan's jacket again. She hated the way lydee treated Jonathan. lydee was so demanding and at times, almost cruel in her teasing. Any time Andie mentioned it, lydee would glare at her for a second then quickly change her expression to one of being hurt because of "*the mean way everyone treats her.*" Total narcissist. Or nutjob. Maybe both.

Andie had noticed that lydee was changing in other ways, too. She wasn't nearly as 'bestie' friends with her, and lydee constantly looked for ways to spew hateful words at their friends, driving most of them away, or heading to the bar for something to drink.

Most of their girlfriends backed off, except for the ones that weren't going to tolerate her messing with their boyfriends. In a matter of days, sometimes hours, the boyfriends would dump the girlfriends to hang out with lydee.

lydee was a weapon of mass destruction.

Andie was determined to enjoy herself at this party, hoping to get past the horrible memory of the club. Kevin never left her side and wouldn't let anyone else dance with Andie. She was good with this; she felt safe with him. Andie also made it a point to avoid lydee and spend time with other friends, agreeing with those who also were sick and tired of lydee's antics.

"Andie, help me find the bathroom," lydee whined, pulling Andie away from Kevin. Actually, she dragged Andie up the stairs and down the hall. Andie figured it was because she was plastered and didn't want to hold her own hair out of the way.

lydee was talking on her phone when she came out of the bathroom. "OH YEAH! Oh, of course we'll come pick you up! Be outside so nobody can stop you!" lydee squealed with delight. "Come on, baby driver, we have more party people to pick up!" tossing the keys in the air.

Andie caught the keys; thankful she had the presence of mind to volunteer to drive instead of letting lydee put everyone's life in jeopardy. Without realizing it, Andie grabbed Jonathan's jacket instead of her own, putting it on as they left.

-... .-.. --- --- -..

Once again, King and his warriors engaged in another battle, the cacophony of clanging metal weapons was deafening…

-... .-.. --- --- -..

Andie had never driven lydee's car, and thank goodness it was an automatic, or they weren't going anywhere. "Sit down, lydee and get your seatbelt on," Andie instructed her tipsy friend. Oddly, lydee obeyed. As they left the driveway, lydee hung out her window singing and screaming at the top of her lungs.

Andie pulled the car over, and scolded, "Dang it lydee, stop it or you're walking back by yourself!"

"Fine, goody two sshoess, have it your way!" slurred lydee while fixing her seatbelt and giving Andie directions to their destination.

They picked up the kid at the first house, and soon arrived at another house to pick up more party goers. Someone brought beers and they weren't shy about passing them around.

Andie insisted they all wear seatbelts. The last thing she needed was for the police to spot underage kids drinking AND driving. lydee cranked the stereo and the noise level shot through the atmosphere. With lydee screaming and playing with the window wipers—and any other button, knob or switch she could reach, including leaning over Andie's lap to play with the light's dimmer—kids screeching like banshees, beer bottles clacking everywhere, Andie couldn't hear her own thoughts, much less the battle going on outside the car.

Andie looked up when she heard the blare of a car horn, just in time to swerve out of the way of the oncoming car. The Aldrich family was going out for ice cream after visiting Katie and Jonathan.

Andie saw fear on the passengers' faces as the cars passed. She over-corrected, hit the curb, and bounced back across the road. Screams erupted from within the cars.

Time crawled through the next few moments. The slow ticking of the second hand echoed through the atmosphere as her eyes took in the details unfolding before her. Slamming head-on into the next car behind the pastor's family, tires screeched, and metal crunched in teeth grinding agony. Windows shattered, sending glass shards flying like surreal snowflakes, and bodies flew through windows. Her body crashed into the steering wheel, flinging her head forward like a wet cloth—the force of the impact caused her to black out.

-... .-.. --- --- -..

A cry of anguish carried out over the battlefield. A battle cry screamed in response. The fighting increased with a determination few had seen in ages. The stakes were high and there wasn't a moment to lose. Devastating loss would occur before this fight was over.

Chapter 10

Consequences

"Can you see if she's breathing?"
"No. Check her pulse…"

"Nothing. Wait, it's there, but it's weak."

"Come on guys, we gotta get her out, she banged her head pretty badly. That cut is gonna need stitches…"

"So, who is first? Them or Andie?" Aimon asked, wiping his hands on his jeans. Emer glanced at Aimon, signaling him to check out the other car, "I'll stay with Andie."

Thyst walked over and crouched down to Emer, hesitating, then stated, "I have good news and bad news, what do you want first?" Groans from the others indicated they didn't care, just say it. "It looks like the other kids were so drunk their bodies didn't have time to brace for the impact. They're gonna have some crazy, awful bruises they won't even remember getting."

"Hey guys! Over here quick!!" Aimon yelled. Phire and Thyst ran over to the other car to help. What they saw stopped them in their tracks. Phire whispered, "Oh, she isn't going to take this well…"

"Stop. You know we can't make judgments like that. You don't know how she will react to finding out what happened," Thyst replied, secretly wanting to trade in the mortal clothes for his battle gear and destroy the evil that caused this tragedy. Their assignment tonight, all they were allowed to do, was to make sure Andie was alive. Anything outside of that was not their mandate.

Emer held Andie as close as he could without causing any more damage to her battered body. Her legs were pinned under the steering wheel from the impact. He gently tried to pull back her hair from the glass embedded in her face. Thankfully, the growing lump on her head was swelling outward and hopefully wouldn't be a severe concussion. He spoke in whispers to her, trying to get a response, while an overwhelming sense of defeat tried to swallow him. "Come on Andie, you can do it, just open your eyes, move something, anything... Come on, remember your training, your King misses you."

It was at this moment that he was thankful for his station in life. He didn't really think he could handle being mortal. A growing realization of King's devotion to his loved ones began to dawn on him. Tears streamed down his face as he softly sang in whispers, gently rocking her close to his chest.

-... .-.. --- --- -..

Darkness again.

Not the cool exhilarating darkness she experienced when King walked her through the heavens. Soul sucking, thick, humid darkness that made her gasp for air and immediately regret her intake because of the sulphuric burn that spread through every fiber of her being.

The hard ground was covered in sharp, jagged rocks cutting into her hands and arms. She tried to stand but had to fight the rising feeling of nausea and the spinning in her head. The rancid scent of death permeated the air. A familiar thought sprang to mind of the time a demon took Jonathan in battle and stabbed him. Yes, that was the smell assaulting her senses.

"*Oh God, where am I?*" she whispered. The dimmest sliver of light began to slide across the horizon. She could see Jonathan standing just across the gorge. He looked sad and relieved at the same time. Why was she sucking in hellish fumes if they were in Covenant?

She became aware of the distance between them. The light didn't reach her. Her heart jumped to her throat with the realization that she wasn't in Covenant, but instead, stranded in the farthest reaches of the valley, and was very much alone.

At least, she hoped she was alone.

Formless shadows in the darkness glared with fiery eyes of hatred, burning into the flesh of her mind. Jagged claws tore at the flesh of her body.

The searing words, from an unknown, invisible source, cut through the fog in her head and split her heart in two, "*YOU* did this. *YOU* killed him. He is *DEAD* and *YOU* are not. You will *beg* for death, that sweet release you hope will stop this torture, but it will only drag you deeper into an abyss *YOU* created and will never escape."

Andie felt her heart banging in her chest like a trapped, frantic animal. Without another thought, she screamed from the depth of her soul.

-... .-.. --- --- -..

The fear that grabbed her throat burst forth from her in a panicked scream as she regained consciousness.

Paramedics jumped back, quickly realizing she had joined them and was in a world of hurt. Calm, soothing words couldn't keep her quiet, so they moved quickly to restrain her on the stretcher to prevent further injury to herself. Her pained cries caused the guy carrying the head end of her stretcher to wonder if her distress was from something other than the physical injury from the impact.

Fear had a stranglehold on her. Upon examination of her breathing, her lungs sounded choked and raspy like the lungs of a lifetime cigarette smoker. Finally, they were able to give her oxygen and something to help her calm down. Emer was there when she opened her eyes, "Shh, be still, you're not alone." She slipped into a restless slumber.

It was a very crowded ambulance ride.

Aimon, Phire and Thyst stayed at the accident site to assist people getting out of the mangled vehicles. Katie was relatively unharmed and had regained consciousness but was sobbing when they tried to get her to vacate the front seat. She had seen Jonathan fly through the windshield and suspected she knew of his condition. Phire supported her while she walked her over to the body of her son lying in the position in which he landed on the ground.

Aimon gently wiped her hair from her face and in doing so, relieved some of the anxiety racing through her thoughts. He gently suggested, "After you are seen at the hospital for treatment, you should visit with King. You will need all the strength you can muster for the days ahead. King is waiting to hold you in his arms to help you through this terrible time. Andie will learn the details in due time. We will do everything in our power to bring her back to Covenant and to restore her relationship with King, and you. She needs you now, more than ever. But, right now, sweet auntie, you need love and support from your King."

Katie's friends from dinner, the Aldrich's, were the ones to call the police at the accident. Mrs. Aldrich volunteered to drive Katie to the hospital while her husband stayed at the scene to pray for those left behind. Donovan couldn't be persuaded to leave his friend's body, and sat close by, crying until the paramedics escorted him away and covered Jonathan's body with a sheet.

Katie was discharged from the emergency room rather quickly, with only scrapes and bruises; better than expected, having survived a fatal accident. As her friend drove her home, they quietly prayed for each other and for the children who lived through the accident. They cried over the loss of Jonathan but tried to reassure each other of his condition being better now. They shared a prayer of hope and strength for Andie during this time of trials. And for Donovan. This was one of the worst things he would have to work through in his young life.

Ruben was waiting at the door for Katie. He walked her inside softly closing the door behind them, hugged her for a moment–careful to not squeeze too tightly–and repeated Aimon's suggestion to spend time with King. She agreed and, leaning on his arm, they walked through the empty house; their footsteps echoing as they entered the darkened library now shrouded in sorrow. He stopped at the door and waited for her to reach the far end of the hallway, then returned to the front of the house to wait.

Back at the scene of the accident, off the side of the road in the dark, three unseen figures adjusted their battle gear, ready to destroy an unseen enemy. A silent nod shared between them, and they were gone. From the flurry of movement in the dark bushes, a demonic screech escaped the throat of an unfortunate being. The hunt was on.

-... .-.. --- --- -..

Just like she had done so many years ago, and as Andie had done recently, Katie stepped through the door. King was there with his arms open wide. Katie melted into his embrace with her heart breaking into a million pieces for both her son and her niece. She dissolved into unashamed tears. King gently kissed her forehead, whispering sweet words of comfort and reassurance. Katie knew she wouldn't see Jonathan while she was there. She would have to wait until the time when she too would never return from the garden.

The sounds of a war in the distance carried on the wind to where they stood. She knew the battle going on was for the lost niece she desperately hoped would find her way back to their King.

After spending time with King and the Father, releasing her hurt and anger, and receiving a flood of love from them, Katie felt a relief that only comes from forgiveness. She would spend more time here until she was ready to go back and work things out in this situation.

She did notice the sounds of battle had subsided considerably. So much warring goes on in the secret places.

-... .-.. --- --- -..

Flashes of light and bursts of sound invaded Andie's consciousness. She could feel the warmth of Emer's touch on her arm, and she once again slipped away into darkness.

The paramedics worked through their protocols, unaware of their extra passenger. Serene calmness saturated the cabin of the ambulance. Exchanging glances, the two medics felt something else was at work here. This girl should be in critical condition based on her injuries, and yet, all her vitals were stable, and she was resting.

They were thankful not to be the ones left behind at the accident. Thoughts of the boy lying dead on the road brought tears they quickly wiped away. Even though they had worked on many scenes like this, they found out this girl was related to the boy and his mother.

It tore at their hearts.

Chapter 11

Aftermath

Shaking involuntarily, Andie couldn't make up her mind if she preferred to be unconscious or awake enough to know what was going on. The emergency room staff had given her pain relievers to help, but having glass pulled from your face and hair just wasn't pleasant. Several of the puncture wounds would require stitches. Others would be fine with butterfly bandages. Then, there was the issue with her legs. They had been pinned in the crash and after the series of x-rays, the doctors were amazed they weren't crushed beyond hope.

Unseen by the hospital staff, a figure stood in the corner, whispering commands into the room's atmosphere. A small voice in her head assured her that no lasting damage would affect her legs. She may have a slight limp at times here in this world, but in Covenant Garden, she was still a mighty leader and would lead a contingent of warriors.

Although that gentle voice only spoke words of hope and affirmation, in her heart she felt worthless and miserable. Horrible thoughts raced through her mind, *"How could I have been so stupid? HOW could I have listened to Iydee, again?! OH MY GOD! What really happened?!"*

Thankfully, someone saw she was in distress again and increased her meds to let her rest. The poor girl has a long road ahead of her.

After a couple of days in the hospital, under doctor's care and police protection, she had recovered enough to be taken to court. As she stood before the judge's bench trembling and covered in bandages and stitches, she desperately wanted a shower. The doctors wouldn't allow her to shower until the wounds on her legs and under her hair healed more completely. They didn't want to risk infection and showering would only irritate her broken skin. Thankfully, a nurse helped her wash her hair with one of those bathing caps.

In her current state of being, she looked more like a lost child–homeless and alone. The judge spoke with authority and compassion. He was the brother of the pastor who witnessed the horrible accident. In the blur of the past few days, several people had testified on behalf of her character and lack of criminal behavior. It seemed she was a victim of circumstance.

It was in the courtroom in front of her parents, along with her sister and Aunt Katie, that Andie learned the details of that fateful night. Even though she tried her best to avoid a collision with the first car, she did in fact, strike the second vehicle with enough force to eject a passenger through the window. The second car was driven by Katie. Jonathan was thrown from the car and died on impact as his body slammed into the ground.

A gasp was heard from the audience and courtroom attendees. Andie's strength drained as she collapsed to the floor. A recess was ordered, and the paramedics tended to Andie. Her family was escorted from the courtroom. Andie would be held in custody until further notice.

The judge allowed Andie to attend the cemetery/burial portion of Jonathan's funeral. Under orders she remained in police custody in the squad car. Tears flowed from her eyes, soaking her shirt. Her anguish-filled sobs caused the two officers to look away from the scene to disguise their emotions.

That night, alone in her cold cell she wept, crying out to God…

A gentle breeze swept through her chamber and as she opened her eyes, her soldiers were there. Phire and Thyst were guarding the door, while Ruben stood in the hall. Emer was kneeling next to her, whispering, "Your King desperately misses you."

Andie tried to argue about being in jail, but Emer laid his hand on her arm and told her to rest. They were not going to leave her alone, and her sleep would open a door of access to the garden.

As Emer sat on the floor next to her bunk, Andie reached out, felt the rugged leather of his armor, and rested her hand on his shoulder.

Aimon's touch on her forehead extinguished the horrific thoughts torturing her mind. While Emer gently whispered calming words of reassurance, she slipped through the veil of consciousness.

On the other side of her blink, she saw him. King was close enough she could feel his breath on her tear-stained face. His face was gentle with tears brimming in his eyes and his touch tender as she fell into his arms crying apologies with great, body shaking sobs. His strength, kindness, and loving words destroyed every remaining doubt of his love. He let her empty herself of all fear and remorse in his loving embrace. He lifted her head to face him and whispered, "I've been waiting for you…"

The coolness of rushing water swept through her sobs, her tears, her heartbeat. Until that moment, she hadn't realized King was singing while they sat in the stream flowing through Covenant. Rushing water, hitting the backside of the giant rock that King reclined against while holding Andie in his embrace, sprayed over them, soaking them in refreshing, soul cleansing showers. She began to feel the release of all the fear and pain from her heart drift away in the water, washing away her tears.

Emer and Phire reached out to hold King's arms and assisted him in standing while he carried Andie out of the water and up the bank of the stream. As he walked, diamond droplets of water from their clothes sent sparkles of rainbows dancing through the air. King stepped beneath the emerald-green canopy of Father's tree, setting Andie down next to the Father.

"This must be your favorite tree," Andie observed, noticing her sword lying beside him.

"Yes, and you are my favorite, too," He replied, welcoming her into his embrace.

Feeling as though a lifetime had passed, after several moments, she began to cry again. She couldn't bring herself to look at Father, but leaned in closer to his chest, and started to apologize.

"Why do you cry? You know you are forgiven. There is no condemnation directed toward you." Father gently questioned.

The calm breeze whispered, *"You are loved, cherished, and restored to the Father."*

King spoke a firm but gentle command, "Andie, you are our loved one and back where you belong with us. As a result of your confession of your frailties, remorse, and acknowledgement of your need for me, you have acquired a fourth stone–the Amethyst of Insight. You realize now that you simply cannot live life on your own terms, but by my strength and grace will you overcome anything that comes against you." It was the deepest, most royal purple stone Andie had ever seen. Nestled firmly in the handle of her sword, it glinted as the sunlight shimmered upon it. The stones lined up along the hilt sent sparks of colored light through the air.

"At the same time," King continued, looking deep into her eyes, "you need to remember your training and resist the enemy. The accuser attacks your thoughts and feelings, and at this difficult time you must be even more vigilant in watching for his attacks. Simply use your weapon, your words, because it is time for you to take up your sword and send the enemy back to the depths. Don't forget, you have a mission to bring others back to the Father. You can't do that if you stay in your misery and pain."

Andie, feeling convicted, but also feeling better about the situation, sat up, wiped her nose on her sleeve, admitting, "Yes, you're right. I do apologize for not paying attention to what was going on with myself." As she sniffled, the thought, "*the accuser...*" raced through her mind. "*Who is the accuser?*" she wondered.

Discernment dawned on her, that all the events as of late, including lydee were in fact, an attack. She could now see that every time she thought about going back to be with King, lydee was there to talk, party, shop, anything to keep her distracted. Deceived. Distanced. "*Good grief...*" she thought dejectedly, her head and shoulders drooped.

King interrupted, "Get up and get your weapon ready for battle."

The soldiers were nearby adjusting their armor and weapons. Emer was smiling and offered his arm to her as they watched her stand up and stretch. Her arms were weak from not being used in battle recently. "Maybe you could use some exercise time with us," Aimon offered, his words always right on the mark. Ruben beat on his chest with a battle cry as Phire and Thyst walked away shaking their heads in amusement.

It was refreshing going through the exercises with the guys, working her muscles back into shape, and recovering her strength. She would have preferred to have stayed there to work out, instead of going back and facing the aftermath of the accident.

For the first time in a long time, she slept peacefully–all night.

-... .-.. --- --- -..

In her cell, Andie woke up and couldn't shake the gut wrenching feeling that accompanies the unknown. *"What would happen to me? How long will I be here? What really happened that night?"*

Questions that begged for answers would have to wait. She had a visitor and was escorted to the visiting room.

Dark, hollow eyes looked over Andie's face searching for a glimmer of hope. Carefully aimed words shot from lydee's mouth and hit Andie's gut like a cannonball, "I can't believe you killed him…"

"What are YOU doing here!?" Andie tried not to scream, still scared of drawing too much attention to herself.

With a mocking gasp, her hand on her partially unbuttoned blouse, lydee's voice took on that annoying whine that only a narcissist can conjure, "Just look what you've done to me. My shoulder is sprained, and all these cuts on my face. Nobody will ever want me."

The slow-motion tilt that accompanies shock swept over Andie and a cool breeze brushed her hair from her face. "*The accuser...*" Those words crept from the front of her brain into her heart. Andie slowly inhaled through her nose, rose from her chair, locked eyes with lydee, and carefully measured her words, "I know exactly WHO you are, WHAT you are, and you can't hurt me anymore."

lydee stopped in mid-sentence, slack jawed at Andie's bold statement. Her black eyes narrowed to stare deep into Andie's soul, and swore an oath that made Andie's skin crawl, "I'm just getting started." lydee stormed out of the room.

The tires spewed gravel as lydee's car screeched to a stop in Katie's driveway. She was on a mission to drive a wedge between Katie and Andie. She had to do everything in her power to keep those two annoying '*loved ones*' from uniting in their assault on her father/leader. She knew what was in store for those who didn't fulfill their sinister mission. Eternal torture was not something she looked forward to enduring.

Her ever-so-stylish heels clacked on the stone steps leading up to the massive front door. After banging on the heavy door, a slight click signaled the bolt sliding back for the door to open.

Ruben met her with a piercing stare that could melt steel, and calmly issued a warning, "Stay away from here, you will not be tolerated, 'ahem,' permitted to trespass on this property again. Any attempt to do so or any attempt to contact the residents will be met with the harshest of punishments allowable under the law of the land." Looking her square in the eye, he reminded her, "I don't live under the laws of this land, and I WILL NOT fail in my mission to destroy you."

Screeching in an unholy tongue, lydee threatened Ruben with curses from the bowels of hell. Ruben bent slightly to get nearly nose to nose with her and said, "... buh-bye."

Shocked, lydee's mouth hung open as he slowly straightened up. Reaching for the door, while maintaining eye contact, he let the door close out the sight of lydee's distorted expression.

The creaking of the door stretched into an eternity of seconds it took to hear the faint '*click*' of the bolt setting shut.

An unearthly scream erupted from lydee... Followed by a myriad of screams from the bowels of hell.

Chapter 12

Destruction and Salvation

Due to unknown forces at work in the situation, all charges against Andie were dropped, except for involuntary manslaughter. This carried a sentence of six months of homebound incarceration. The Court assigned Katie custody of Andie for the duration of the homebound period. Uneasy relief washed over the courtroom. Andie's parents were thankful for the sentencing but questioned the reasoning behind it. The judge assured them he felt this was in the best interests of all parties involved.

"*All parties involved…*" the words tumbled in Andie's mind. All she could imagine was a period of time being trapped in the house with the mother of the person she killed. Her favorite aunt was heartbroken and cried openly. Emotions swept over Andie, stabbing at her heart, burning her eyes, and drowning out all thought processes. She was escorted from the courtroom to a cell to await processing.

Sitting in silence while her parents and Katie took care of paperwork and made arrangements with the probation officer who would oversee her homebound time, Andie took a moment to close her eyes. She whispered to the person she knew would be listening. A gentle rush of coolness washed over her, causing her to relax. Nagging darts of doubt tried to dig their way back into her soul, but a small flash of light reminded her to combat those lies with her weapon—her words filled with hope and love from her King. She couldn't see him, but she knew he was sitting next to her, with her soldiers standing guard nearby.

An officer came to collect Andie and took her to the car with Katie. A car had been loaned to Katie until the insurance company settled the case with the accident. Katie and Andie were the only passengers and neither one spoke during the drive.

A police car escorted them home. Soft music streamed from the radio and floated through the open windows. This was one of their favorite pastimes, just riding in the car with the music turned up and windows rolled down, dreaming of far-off places, or singing along with the songs. Katie knew all the words to all the songs—even the songs Andie was shocked to find Katie remembered from her past.

What Andie would give to go back to the past, anything to erase the overwhelming pain clutching her chest. She could not imagine what Katie was going through. *"Sweet Katie. How could something like this ever happen to her? How could I be responsible for hurting someone I love so much?"* Questions like jagged daggers took aim at her mind. A flash of light from a passing car quelled those fiery darts in her thoughts and she silently offered a thankful prayer.

Arriving at the house, they saw Ruben outside sweeping the porch—again. *"Poor Ruben,"* Andie thought, *"he was supposed to come here and learn more about how we are to act like King, and if nothing else, I've shown him exactly how to do the opposite."* She lowered her gaze when he looked at her. Ruben rushed to help them by opening the door and searched their faces for any possible conversation. Other than a polite "thank you," nothing else was offered.

The officer attached the device to Andie's ankle, explaining to her the requirements and expectations of said device. A transmitter in the device would relay her position to a WiFi like box in the center of the house to give her room to move about freely. But it would closely restrict her outside adventures. The house was enormous and didn't leave much range for the outside. Thankfully, it would allow some movement in the garden close to the house, and the kitchen and front porches, but nothing else. She was given stern warnings for violating the terms of the agreement, crossing the lines of restriction and any attempt at removal of the device.

Katie thanked the officers for their help, took down the emergency phone numbers and assured them there would be no issues concerning the probation or device. She shook their hands and closed the door behind them as they left. A solemn silence fell over the house.

Andie headed to her room, absorbing the overwhelmingly loud echo of silence.

She passed Jonathan's room, stopped, and looked back to see his room had been cleaned up and curtains opened. Bone crushing sorrow in her chest wrenched her heart and made her stomach ache. *"He was so young, smart, and funny,"* flashes of memories flooded her mind, *"He could figure out how to do anything if someone showed an interest."*

Her stomach turned over and she headed to the bathroom. Grabbing a washcloth to rinse off her face, then placing it on her neck, she noticed his things had been removed from the cabinets. Looking through the closet, his favorite beach towel and other items were gone. Andie wondered if Katie had done this to make it easier for herself or for Andie's sake. An overpowering surge of sorrow grabbed her by the throat and flooded her eyes. She cried out and rushed to her room sobbing quietly.

Ruben paced the entry foyer, completely discombobulated. He couldn't understand why this had him so rattled. He was a warrior. Many victories came from his battle axe and determination. But this situation was out of his realm of understanding. "*Why does this hurt?*" he wondered, "*What is the purpose of all this pain?*" It began to anger him, and yet when he heard Andie cry out near the bathroom upstairs, his heart crumbled.

Katie had poured a glass of iced tea and went to the library to collect her senses. She was in no condition to talk with anyone, but she knew they could not continue to live in silence. Andie had to know she was still a part of this family, and Ruben, like it or not, was also a part of the family.

Her heart ached for her son. She had cleaned up his room and put away some of his things. She halfway thought it would be easier if his things were out of sight, but there sat his favorite chair. It would not be easy to ignore. Instead, it almost demanded an explanation for the absence of Jonathan.

She looked around and saw many of the projects he and Donovan had worked on, model cars and other things that kept them learning were strewn around the tabletops as if they had just gone to another room.

Her eyes watered with stinging tears as she spotted his sword in its place next to hers. The crushing realization that he would never again use it was the final straw in her maintaining self-control. She wept inconsolably.

Time marched on as the slow, methodical ticking of the grandfather clock in the foyer kept time with each member of the house fighting their own silent battle.

Hours passed slowly with the changing shadows of the afternoon. The world outside moved forward with unstoppable momentum, oblivious to the devastation inside. A gentle breeze swept through the open windows, causing the curtains to undulate–trying to stir up movement, some sign of life, anything to break this curse of sorrow.

-... .-.. --- --- -..

Dread crawled up her back with its sharp, bloody claws stabbing into her brain.

-... .-.. --- --- -..

Andie's thoughts were a flurry of fearful rejection and possible hatred from the one person in her life she had devastated in the most horrific of ways. How could she apologize for killing Jonathan? Although she wasn't deliberately responsible, she was liable for his death. Would she have to move back home after the homebound period? Would she ever be comfortable in this home knowing Jonathan would never be here again? Would Donovan's parents hate her for causing their son so much pain and anguish, as well? What would her own parents do or think? Her sister hadn't spoken to her since the accident.

-... .-.. --- --- -..

The claws twisted and dug deeper. A sinister chuckle whispered in her ear. She could feel her heartbeat racing again.

-... .-.. --- --- -..

Oh geesh, what about school? Her junior year would end at home, summer would come and go, then her senior year would begin. A flash of white light caught her attention.

She stopped and took a deep breath, relaxed her shoulders, and whispered, "Thank you for the strength, grace, and favor I will need over the next few weeks, months, and well, for the rest of my life. My strength comes from you, my King, and I trust you have the details sorted out."

Her fists and arms flexed as if holding a heavy object, then relaxed. Holding her arms out front, palms facing away (in a STOP position), she delivered a crushing blow to the enemy grating on her brain, "Enemy of the King, you will LEAVE ME ALONE! My King has said that you must flee when I, in his authority, resist your attacks!" With a quick shove in the empty air, she gave out a forceful command, "LEAVE!"

She flopped over on her bed, exhausted, but decided to get a glass of chocolate milk. It was good for headaches.

She realized she was tip toeing as she descended the stairs. Why was she still so apprehensive? Oh yeah, she hadn't stopped and talked things over with Katie. She still felt like she shouldn't be here, and yet, under court orders, she HAD to be here. You know that gut twisting moment when you know you must do something, but you do everything you can to avoid it? Yeah, that's what she'd been doing. The stomach butterflies were going full force and she could feel her heartbeat start racing again. "Nope, I gotta talk to Katie, Ruben, or somebody. This is ridiculous," she announced to nobody in particular.

-... .-.. --- --- -..

"Katie will never forgive you," a repulsive voice whispered.

-... .-.. --- --- -..

"SHUT UP, I already dealt with you!" she commanded, to everybody listening. She knew they were listening. Listening for the slightest excuse to jump back in and torment her head and heart again. She knew she had to carefully guard her words and thoughts. But right now, she really needed that chocolate milk.

Ruben didn't know what to do with himself. There are only so many times you can take out the trash, sweep the porches, and pull weeds in the garden. He knew what needed to be done, but this had to be a personal decision on Andie's part. Or Katie's part. Neither one had spoken more than just obligatory niceties in passing to each other. Each was unsure how to interact with the other. Andie wondered if Ruben had lost all respect for her as a warrior, and whether her relationship with Katie would ever be restored. Katie worried about whether Andie would be hostile for being trapped in this house with her. Ruben was at his wits end. If it weren't for the times he could talk to the King in the garden, he would have given up his post.

And then, as if by divine appointment, the three converged at the bottom of the stairs. Ruben spoke first, "I have a massive, newfound respect for both of you ladies. I never in my wildest dreams would have ever been able to imagine a situation like this, and yet here we are," waving his arms wide.

Katie and Andie looked at each other, tears burning their eyes and hearts breaking. A soft breeze blew through the open windows, gently billowing the sheer curtains again, racing through the foyer and swirling around the trio. An eternity ticked by measured by the grandfather clock.

Tick ... tock ... tick ... tock ...

As the two ladies reached for each other, foregoing wiping the tears in their eyes, they embraced, and cried apologies of remorse while reassuring the other they still loved them more than they would ever know. Ruben was spent, he bent over, put his hands on his knees and sniffled. He didn't dare let Katie and Andie see it, but when they pulled him into their embrace, he openly wept. Big, fat manly tears flowed freely. He truly was learning how the King loved his family.

-... .-.. --- --- -..

Immediately, the garden battlefield erupted into cries of victory and triumph. Once again, King leaned back against his Father's tree, and exhaled a sigh of relief. The lady warriors had done it, they had overcome the battle the enemy had waged between the two of them.

-... .-.. --- --- -..

Onto the handle of Andie's sword, a fifth stone, a Sapphire, representing focus and self- discipline, settled into place.

-... .-.. --- --- -..

The house shrugged off the shroud of sorrow that clung so tightly to its walls. The clock in the foyer chimed in a slightly higher tone. Squirrels and birds sprang to life in the garden, chasing each other with chattering taunts. Fresh air blew through the windows reminding them of the newly flowering rose bushes along the entry and back doors. Andie couldn't be sure, but it felt like the earth shifted on its axis.

Something had definitely changed.

Without a moment's hesitation, she suggested, "I need to go back to Covenant, I must talk with King."

Ruben agreed, and Katie offered to get an early supper on the table. It had been an exhausting week and truthfully, she just wanted pizza, and might as well mix up some brownies.

Ruben secretly did a fist pump at the news of brownies. Katie smiled, shaking her head at the thought of this warrior craving chocolate.

Running to the door in the library, Andie stopped and wondered about the ankle device. Calling out to Ruben and Katie, "Hey guys, what do you think about this thing? Will it be ok?"

The others stepped back into the foyer, looking at each other in agreement, and responded, "It should be fine, if not, we'll just report it as an *'oops, first time'* to the officer."

Not wasting a second, Andie bolted for the door. She spied all three swords standing at attention as she passed through the welcoming warmth of the library and abruptly stopped at the door.

A lifetime of memories flashed through her mind as she reached for the ancient brass knob. A stab of pain poked at her heart, but pushing it aside she entered the hall, anticipating the sweet air from Covenant to fill her lungs once again.

Approaching the far end of the darkness, the crystal doorknob awaited her command to open and upon the touch of her fingers, did so. True to form and far surpassing her expectations, her return was highlighted with a flurry of emotions–blissful elation and painful remorse. Pushing all those conflicting emotions aside, she ran to her King, throwing her arms around him in an embrace.

Chapter 13

The War for a Single Soul

Laughter and tears flowed freely between Andie and King. Cheers erupted all around from the warriors returning from battle. A gentle breeze engulfed them while strolling arm in arm over to Father's tree and visiting with him in an ecstatic reunion.

They spent many hours talking about things to come, and Andie assured them they could depend on her to fulfill her mission to help bring the loved ones back to Covenant and in relationship with King and Father. They smiled lovingly at her confession and affirmed their belief in her determination to do so.

In the following weeks, Andie spent more time in training and visiting with King than at home doing schoolwork. Katie was ok with this. It also gave her time to adjust to life in a 'new normal' way that she never would have dreamed. Ruben stayed with Katie, just as a support element, realizing that grief can be overwhelming and so much stronger than he ever could have guessed.

Mrs. Aldrich, Donovan's mother, visited frequently with Katie, talking and listening. More listening than talking.

She did share that she was becoming concerned for Donovan. "He spends most of his time in his room, even sometimes missing supper. His attitude is somber, and he finds no joy in his regular pastimes. Unfortunately, most of them had involved Jonathan, and now, Donovan has just given up," Mrs. Aldrich divulged, not wanting to detract from Katie's sorrow, but genuinely concerned for her young son.

Katie quickly recognized the beginning signs of depression and suggested, "Let's specifically pray for his safety and sanity. This event has taken almost everyone hostage to grief. I can't bear the thought of another son being lost in this manner."

-... .-.. --- --- -..

Katie taught Ruben how to cook; and while covered in flour, tomato sauce, and who knows what else, he presented lasagna with garlic bread. Accolades of, "That was amazing, Ruben!" caused him to beam with delight. Andie and Katie were pleasantly surprised to find out that he could cook very well, indeed. He gave a slight bow in response.

During supper with Ruben and Andie that night, Katie shared what she had learned from Mrs. Aldrich about Donovan. Leveling her gaze at Andie, she suggested, "You should talk with King and find out what exactly can be done to help Donovan."

Andie agreed, "I promise to bring it up the next time I see him."

Although there was a renewed sense of peace throughout the house, and each person had found ways to adapt and recover from the turmoil of the past, a small nagging dart was beginning to demand attention.

Skipping dessert and end of semester homework, Andie decided to spend time with King. She longed for the days of laughter and joy she enjoyed in Covenant. But knowing there was danger in store for her young friend, she was determined to find out what she could do to help.

The air was tense as she stepped through the door. Still sunny and peaceful, there was a sense of foreboding lurking around every tree, boulder, and thought that entered her mind.

She found King with the Father under the emerald canopy, right where she knew to find them. As she sat down with them, King slipped his arm around her shoulder and gently hugged her. Andie would never tire of this moment, the fragrant floral scent of the garden mixing with the distinctive, pleasant aroma that emanated from King was both invigorating and relaxing.

Feeling the nagging tug in her heart, Andie asked, "What is going on with Donovan? Katie says his mom is worried about him and they are concerned that he is becoming depressed."

A slight shift trembled through the ground as King turned to face her. Tears formed in his eyes.

"It's true, Donovan is having trouble dealing with the loss of his best friend." King answered, nodding to the thickening darkness sneaking around the corner of the far end of the garden. "There is a battle going on for his very life, and he isn't as strong as Jonathan was in his battle skills. He is desperately in need of help." King looked deep into Andie's eyes, blinking back tears.

"OK, so if he needs help, then why aren't you there, helping him?!" Andie questioned, startled by her own accusation.

"Don't be so quick to judge that I am not there. You should know that I am with him as well as with you. That was my promise to all my loved ones. But I cannot move on his behalf if he doesn't call me, or in my authority, call his warriors who are standing with him. He has instead listened to the destructive lies of the tormentor that wants to destroy him and his family." He pointed across the valley, "That darkness on the horizon will overtake him tonight if he doesn't pull through this battle victorious."

Panic gripped her throat, making her words sound squeaky, "What can I do to help?"

Waves of emotions rolled over her heart as King began to speak and assure her, "As one of his closest friends, you must go to battle for him, you must find the words he needs to hear to bring him back to us and heal his brokenness. This is the moment for which you've trained."

"Sure, but these jelly legs aren't gonna help me…" she thought to herself.

Father and King smiled and that's when she remembered they could hear her thoughts. "Please guide my every word and action as I try to help Donovan. I'm not even sure how to start, I am stuck at home with the ankle device," Andie reminded King.

Still smiling as they stood up, King placed his hands on her shoulders and stated, "You still have much to learn, and now, you'll find that you too can move through the atmosphere in ways you've never realized. Remember when I took you to the mountaintop, then stood on the beach, and finally, floated in the spacious reaches of the universe? That is available to you as well, I'll show you when the time comes. But for now, you need to muster your troops and prepare your heart for a time of testing, tears, and triumph. You must not lose this battle, Andie. A soul hangs in the balance. Every demon in the enemy's army will try to destroy you and Donovan. Do not back down."

"*No pressure*," she thought as her stomach flopped around.

"Yes, it is all pressure, but I know you will be victorious. I've already defeated the enemy. You have to remind him and Donovan of that fact," King reminded Andie.

Andie turned, and as always, Emer was right at her elbow. "Guys, we have to help Donovan," she announced as she looked each one in the eye. Without hesitation, they nodded in agreement.

"Say the word, Andie, we're ready to go," Emer responded, speaking for the group, including Ruben. "He didn't want to miss out on this battle," Ruben nodded, winked, and smiled as he gave a quick swing of his battle ax.

"This is a battle with two fronts, Andie," King stated, motioning to the valley in front of them. Battalions of soldiers were in formation. "Here, and in the moment of time and space where your friend is hurting and considering ending his life to escape the pain that is stealing his heart. You will travel between here in the garden and there with Donovan in your heart and mind. Everything you say there will have an effect here. Using your weapon—your words—to speak my truth to his heart, will also wage war here. I will be with you there and watch the battle here. I trust you to do what needs to be done. I trust you with his life." His loving eyes were wet again but smiling with anticipation.

Swallowing the lump in her throat, she relaxed her shoulders and exhaled, "Ok, here we go. Guys, we have to bring back our loved one…"

The soldiers were in formation around her as they ran to the battleground. Andie stumbled and lurched forward, almost falling, but realized she landed astride Phire's back. A lack of armor on the back made it possible to carry someone without injuring them. She only needed a moment to shake the shattered thoughts free from her mind to signal she was ready. Phire straightened up as she pushed off and ran beside him.

The coppery scent of blood hung thick in the air, but she pushed back the fear and rising threat of nausea in her pursuit of victory over the treacherous enemy. She was confident in the knowledge that she had all she required to fulfill her objective. Her King had supplied for every need; and her soldiers anticipated any unexpected need for assistance.

Closing in on the front lines of the battle, she moved with cat-like silence, easing into position with her soldiers. The cover of darkness aided them in moving around, but darkness was not their preference.

Andie noticed the glowing pearl moon over the valley. The battalions of soldiers were ready for battle. The creak of leather and armor caused Andie to grimace. Utmost silence was needed to maintain their advantage. She was determined to keep the upper hand and ultimately the victory in this battle.

A trickle of sweat rolled past her eye, catching a glint of moonlight; her concentration focused on the open field before them. Being newly promoted in this regiment and knowing what was at stake, she knew she couldn't let her mind wander.

A slight sound to her left caught her attention. King smiled, as he was practically nose-to-nose with her. He whispered, "Go, and help him." He waved his arm in front of her, opening a portal through which she and her soldiers stepped onto the top of the school building where Donovan stood dangerously close to the edge of the roof.

Consumed with grief, he didn't realize Andie had joined him. Her soldiers lined up with Donovan's soldiers, surrounding the young man, ready to move into action. Now with Andie there, something could be done to help him. She could speak words bringing help from the furthest reaches of eternity.

A cool wind wafted over the rooftop. Andie relaxed her shoulders and whispered, "Donovan, I'm here. Please talk to me." Waiting for a response, she figured he didn't hear her. She began to repeat herself when she saw a salty tear glistening in the moonlight roll down his cheek. She stopped herself as Donovan turned slightly and tried to speak.

At first, he was somber and pathetic; and in the next blink, he was screaming in her face, "HOW COULD YOU DO THIS!? HOW COULD YOU KILL MY BEST FRIEND!? HOW STUPID COULD YOU BE!?" He started to punch at her, but hesitated.

Andie's heart crumbled. She could see the absolute devastation on this young man's face. His heart was smashed to oblivion, and it was her fault.

-... .-.. --- --- -..

The sounds of battle raged from the garden valley. Screams of anger filled the air.

-... .-.. --- --- -..

She turned her shoulder to him and said, "Go on, hit me; punch me. I know you want to. You gotta get all that hurt out of you. Go on, punch me." She patted her arm near the shoulder, "In the shoulder. In the arm. In the gut. Whatever you need to get this all out." She braced herself for the rain of hits she anticipated.

Nothing.

Nothing but heart wrenching sobs from his shaking body. She looked at Emer; his eyes were attentive, awaiting a command. Looking around at the rest of them, they were alert to every word being said, and most were also moved with compassion.

The gentle breeze ruffled Donovan's hair and cooled his tears.

Andie reached for his arm, but he pulled away from her and dropped to his knees. "I can't bear the thought of trying to get through this summer. We were supposed to go camping on our own for the first time, or... or... or... getting through high school, getting our first jobs, planning our futures…" His voice trailed off as he held his head in his hands. Andie knew they were thinking about joining the military and serving their country like their fathers had done in their youth.

Andie sat down on the pebble studded rooftop, crossed her legs, and reached her arm around his shoulders. His body slumped onto hers and his sobbing shook both their bodies.

She had to force herself to speak in calming tones to keep herself from crying, "Someone needs to hear your story, in your words. They are going through stuff and need to know that someone like them was able to overcome the struggle. It's your choice. Jonathan didn't have a choice, but you can choose to run to your parents for support and love, or you can crush them with the decision to leave this life."

Andie waited for a response that didn't come, and continued, "Do you hear the battle raging in your head and clawing at your heart? Do you hear it? Are you willing to give in to it and let the enemy devour you? There will be never-ending torment and anguish for your parents if you decide to kill yourself. They may come to terms with the loss, but you will leave a giant hole in their hearts that will never completely heal."

Andie paused, checking to see if he was listening, then continued, "Or you can fight. You can fight back against the darkness trying to extinguish your light, your story, your purpose. Fight it! Fight it with your words! **Fight for your life!** This is your moment of victory! Do you want to lose everything now, or do you want to fight back and pull out of the pit of hell that threatens to swallow you? Fight back Donovan, it's your choice! If you want to fight, you have all the backup you need. They're here with us, but you must make the decision to fight now! Say the words—use your weapon and strike back. Once you start, you cannot fail, but you have to start and keep on fighting until you break through!" Sweat streamed down her face.

-... .-.. --- --- -..

Clanging metal screeched through air thick with the stench of sweat and hate.

-...  --- --- -..

The barest cool breeze swirled around them. She looked for a response from him, waiting to hear anything, but also ready to pull him back if he tried to jump.

Donovan couldn't see this, but there were no less than four pairs of hands holding onto him. Along with two soldiers standing guard, two more on the ground below.

Andie gently rocked him in her arms and silently whispered a prayer. Stroking his jet-black hair back from his face, she could see a peace settling on his countenance. She smiled knowing that King was talking to him in his heart and loving him just as he had promised.

Someone driving past the school had seen two people on the rooftop and called the police. Andie could see the lights that lit up the police car headed their way. Kissing the top of his head, she pushed him up to face him, "Donovan, I can tell you've changed your mind, but you need to speak the words out loud. I'll help you if you want."

He nodded in agreement, and she could hear from the other realm a scream of victory rising over the battle valley. "Repeat after me, 'I choose life. I choose to trust in my King and the Father—and their love for me. I choose to take back all that was stolen from me by the enemy. I refuse to listen to that filthy liar who has been exposed and has been defeated! I stand against you and your lies. I resist your attack on my life! Leave me alone now, in the name of my King!'"

Donovan spoke quietly at first but more forcefully when it got deep into his heart. He wasn't gonna just roll over and die. Nope.

"We gotta go, now." Andie directed as they vanished from the rooftop and appeared on the battleground. The joyous cacophony of victory assaulted their ears when they arrived, and it was a glorious thing. They flopped down on the grass and laughed until they cried with relief.

-... .-.. --- --- -..

The two officers had the spotlight trained on the rooftop as they approached from the parking lot. Upon reaching the roof, they found it vacant except for a small scattering of feathers.

Stumbling over his words, the first officer questioned, "Did I imagine it? I could have sworn I saw two people up here."

The second officer turned, looked him in the eye and shook his head. He picked up a feather on the way back down from the roof.

-... .-.. --- --- -..

King was laughing as he reached for Andie's hand and pulled her close. He kissed her forehead, as was his custom, and thanked her profusely. "I knew you could reach him. I knew he would listen to you. Thank you for bringing him home."

She was crying again. As strong as she thought she was, King had a way of bringing her to tears. Happy tears. Tears of joy that strengthened her resolve to do anything he asked.

In the days that followed, Mrs. Aldrich would stop in and check on Katie, but Katie always turned the attention back to Donovan, "How's he doing? He is more than welcome to come and visit. Maybe he would like to collect some of his items he has left over here. No, come to think of it, if he wants, he can leave them here and use them when he visits."

Breathing a sigh of relief, Mrs. Aldrich smiled, "He has been asking if it would be ok to come and visit with you all, but he wanted me to ask first. He really misses Jonathan, but he likes Andie and *loves* your brownies. You gotta give me that recipe. So, if it's ok, I'll tell him he can come over and 'hang out' with you." Katie and Andie laughed, it was fun watching Mrs. Aldrich and the relaxed personality she had picked up while spending time at Katie's house since Donovan returned.

Everyone who spent a good deal of time at Katie's house ended up much happier than when they arrived. There was a supernatural atmosphere of joy and peace that surrounded the inhabitants and visitors. At times, Andie wondered if Covenant Garden was beginning to infiltrate the house. That would suit her just fine.

This house was her refuge, her place of adventure and most definitely her home. She never wanted to leave—and if it was up to her, she never would.

Chapter 14

The Invitation

Kevin came over to see Andie after several weeks to check on her. Once again, he met Ruben at the door, "Hi there, do you remember me? I brought Andie home one night and…" He was not prepared for the mountain of Ruben to reach out and pat him on the shoulder with the battle-hardened hand of friendship.

"Of course, I know you, Kevin. You were truly a hero that night. I want to be sure to let you know that you are welcome here anytime you like." Ruben's voice boomed like thunder when he forgot to tone it down. "'Ahem,' anytime you like." He repeated a little softer.

Kevin, wide eyed and stone faced, remained rooted to the front porch. A slight pull on his shoulder from Ruben was all it took to uproot him, and they went to the kitchen to announce his arrival.

Andie was setting the *'still hot out of the oven, don't touch them, Ruben'* brownies on the hot mat on the counter and turned to give Kevin a quick hug. Stepping back from him, she realized he was still in shock, "Ruben takes some getting used to. Don't worry, he's a teddy bear." Andie offered. *"In reality, he's a grizzly bear. Not to be trifled with..."* she thought to herself. Ruben turned to her and winked.

Then reaching for the brownies, Ruben saw Kevin's eyes go wide again as Katie smacked at Ruben's hand.

"Oh no, that can't be good." Kevin thought in a tangle of emotions ranging from *'that's-awesome!* to *what's-the-quickest-way-out-of-here?'* panic.

Katie was making dinner for the Aldrich family's visit and suggested to Andie to invite Kevin to stay for dinner as well. Nodding in agreement, Andie rushed back to the dining room with another stack of plates to set on the table.

Kevin and Ruben were savoring the tiniest pieces of brownie that Katie had cut for them. The delectable chocolate treat was not to be gulped down at once. No, it deserved to be enjoyed slowly and thoughtfully.

They jumped when she spoke.

"Geesh! Don't sneak up like that!" Kevin squeaked around the bite of heavenly chocolate goodness. Ruben's brownie disappeared into thin air like a puff of smoke.

Watching their faces change from expressions of bliss to startled was too much for Andie. She burst out laughing, and after catching her breath, she invited Kevin to stay for dinner.

After exchanging glances with a still astonished Ruben looking for his brownie, Kevin accepted but needed to call home and let them know where he would be. Permission was granted and Kevin offered to help with setting the table.

Introductions were made as the Aldrich family arrived; and Donovan and Kevin knew each other already, so there wasn't any awkwardness that accompanied new acquaintances. The talk around the table was lighthearted and enjoyable.

Kevin could not figure out how everyone was getting along so well but kept it to himself. It totally confused him how they could visit with no feelings of blame or anger at the situation that had affected both families.

After eating dinner and clearing the table, Katie, and the Aldrich's, retired to the front living room with coffee while Andie, Donovan, and Kevin wandered off to the library still laughing and having a great time.

"Can I ask a question?" asked Kevin.

"You just did." Donovan shot back.

"Stop it, goofball," Andie punched Donovan's shoulder. He tumbled into Jonathan's favorite chair. "Go on, Kevin."

"First, thanks for inviting me tonight. I had a great time. Really, I did. But I can't help but wonder," Kevin started, but stopped as he saw Andie and Donovan glance at each other. "I don't want to bring up any sore spots," pausing again to read the room, "but HOW can you all get along after what happened to Jonathan?" The words quickly spilled out.

Quietness hung in the room. A cloud of unspoken words waited patiently for their chance to be released. Lots of fidgeting, adjusting positions in the chairs, and clearing of throats broke the silence.

"I wished it had been me instead," whispered Donovan, his eyes red and wet.

"I'm thankful it wasn't," Andie spoke softly, "I don't know how anyone can come to terms with losing a child, but I think your mother might have lost her grip. I know Katie almost did."

Grandfather Clock chimed the half hour. Ceiling high bookcases stood obediently, awaiting someone to browse their stuffed shelves. Breezes once again swirled under the curtains billowing in the open windows. Laughter from the other room rang out, disturbing the somber mood of the trio.

Unseen to them, an entire garden valley hung on every word spoken in the library. Would the responses be full of anger, hurt and disappointment, or words of comfort and peace?

Andie turned to face both the guys and began to lay out the story of how she came to live with Katie. She succinctly addressed the history of her parent's divorce, losing her best friend, and her first boyfriend all in a short period of time.

Thankfully, she landed here with Katie and Jonathan. Although she loved her parents and sister, she felt more at home in this awe-inspiring dwelling than with her own family. She finally understood why she was given permission to explore the secret rooms tucked away in plain sight.

Donovan knew about the door in the library because Jonathan had shared with him the wonders that lay beyond waiting to be discovered personally. Donovan had also entered the door here and spent time in Covenant, at Jonathan's invitation.

Andie and Donovan looked at each other, then looked at Kevin. Maybe they should talk about some of the other items in the library first. There were swords and armor, along with giant framed letters written in *"what's that crazy word"* fancy writing.

Donovan showed Kevin the model he and Jonathan were working on. Tears formed in his eyes. As he wiped those eyes, Andie spoke up, "There are some things that we just can't explain, but if you're truly sincere in wanting to know how we can still love each other after what I did…" her voice trailed off. Donovan wrapped his arms around her.

Kevin was walking around the room inspecting the swords, amazed at the startling bright jewels in the hilts of each one. He gave up trying to read the calligraphy housed in golden frames and looked at the many family pictures lined up on the shelves.

"Shouldn't you people hate each other? I mean, Donovan, you were best friends with Jonathan." Then turning to Andie, "Your own cousin is dead because of that accident." Kevin slapped his hand over his mouth as the words escaped.

Donovan hugged Andie tighter. She cried. He cried. Kevin cried. "Oh my gosh, I am so sorry. I just don't understand. I wish I could, but I don't." he confessed.

Moments ticked by with Grandfather Clock. The house groaned as it settled.

Andie whispered a short prayer under her breath. Donovan sat down, blowing his nose on tissues from the table. He missed the trash basket. Kevin dropped to his knees and begged for forgiveness.

She smiled as she wiped a stray piece of hair out of his eyes. It reminded her of someone else whose hair did the same. Emer had been her shadow through so much of the past stretch of time, good grief, how long had it been? She moved in right before Christmas break and ventured through the door not long after. It was now close to the end of summer. It had been less than a year and yet she felt many years older.

Andie hadn't really given much thought to telling Kevin about King. And yet, that was part of her mission. *"I really wish I had talked to King about this before now, what should I say, how do I break the crazy news to him that I fight demonic monsters hell bent on killing me?"*

Donovan read her mind and nodded. Setting his chin on his hand, almost teasing her in a brotherly fashion, "Go on, Andie, tell him about the door."

All eyes slowly landed upon the non-descript door standing in the corner of the magnificent library. Once again, it seemed out of place here, but usually those are the best places to visit, the ones that take you by surprise.

"How long ago was it for you, Donovan?" Andie asked.

"About two years ago. Things have never been the same. I wish I had paid more attention to all that King had told me while I was there. I must admit, it had been some time between visits when this happened with Jonathan. That could be why I didn't handle things well," Donovan admitted.

Kevin sat on the floor, looking at the two of them chattering on about this *"King"* person. "Are you gonna tell me anything or not? Do I have to get up and go through there myself, or are you gonna keep jabbering like crazy people?" He stood up. Andie and Donovan jumped up as well.

"There is no way in the world we can say anything to prepare you for what you'll see, hear, or do… or who you will meet. Just know that once you go through that door, you will never be the same and eventually you'll understand why we are the way we are." Andie cautioned, holding Kevin's arm.

"You certainly won't forget it. Or regret it." Donovan pledged.

Kevin thought about it for a minute and decided, "I have to know. I have to see for myself."

"We'll be right here, waiting for you."

As he reached for the brass doorknob, a small spark jumped to his fingers. Soundlessly the knob turned, and the door opened to the same dark hallway.

Andie and Donovan waited by the door, listening for any sound. After several '*oops*' and '*oh, come on*' from Kevin, they heard the crystal knob squeak slightly, then the sweetest sound in all of heaven and earth reached their ears.

"I've waited so long to meet you..."

Click

-... .-.. --- --- -..

Biography

Ms. Alexander was born in 1967 in Kingsville, Texas, and named after the Mouseketeer, Annette Funicello.

Annette has lived many lives as a college student, computer artist, military Family Readiness Group advocate and leader, photographer, and voice actor ("Your voice is least annoying. You've got the job").

Being a single mother for the past 15 years, she has worked as a substitute teacher while her children where in school. It was during this time, the idea for a story came to her and she started chronicling the adventures in **Blood Garden**.

She lives in Waxahachie, Texas, with her youngest daughter Rebecca, who shares her artistic and creative tendencies. They are planning many books and art endeavors together.

When asked what her superpowers would be? —A Linguist Wordsmith. She wants to understand, read, write, and speak all the languages in the world. Even the dead ones. It sounds like fun!

Speaking of languages, if you were wondering, this [-... .-.. --- --- -..] is Morse Code for blood.

Made in the USA
Coppell, TX
12 November 2021